GRRRRwoooofff!!

Benji woofed sheepishly, his grin becoming silly around the whiskers ... who was that fluffy white dog nosing in *his* bin?

Benji belonged to no one but everybody loved this shaggy, friendly creature. Each morning Benji raced through town, wagging his tail in joy, greeting all his friends with a loud woof, and calling for breakfast at Paul and Cindy's house.

One day things began to happen. Benji found Tiffany, a dog beautiful beyond his wildest dreams. Then sinister intruders broke into Benji's secret hideout. Paul and Cindy were in terrible danger ... and the only one who could save them was Benji!

BENJI

*For other titles in the Target series
see end pages*

BENJI

Based on the original film script by Joe Camp

ALLISON THOMAS

A TARGET BOOK
published by
the Paperback Division of
W. H. ALLEN & Co. Ltd

First published in the U.S.A.
by Pyramid Books, Pyramid Communications, Inc.

First published in Great Britain
by Tandem Publishing Ltd, 1976

Second impression 1978

Copyright © 1975
by American Broadcasting Company Merchandising, Inc.

Printed in Great Britain by
Richard Clay (The Chaucer Press) Ltd., Bungay, Suffolk
for the publishers, W. H. Allen & Co. Ltd,
44 Hill Street, London W1X 8LB

ISBN 0 426 11551 1

For Thommy,
Diamond Dog

ONE

The morning sun was trying hard to shine in through the windows of the house, but the house was very old and nobody had washed its windows in more than forty years. So, instead of coming in, the sun bounced off the dusty glass, and the windows looked as though the light was pouring *out* from *inside* the house. But the lower corner of one of the panes on the second floor was broken, and the sunshine managed to work its way inside and wake up Benji.

Benji's face appeared at the broken window. His nose twitched with excitement as he checked out the day. The sunshine that had awakened him and that now warmed his body was his first clue, but the morning breezes brought more information to his little black nose. The smell of a beautiful day in early summer came to him – sunshine on the grass, and the scent of flowers opening to the morning, of cows in their pastures – all of these fine odours made Benji eager to be out enjoying the day. Most of all, he thought he could smell breakfast somewhere in the distance, and this smell called to him even more strongly than the grass and the flowers.

Yawning, and shaking his ears to clear the last sleepiness from his head, Benji wiggled through the hole in the window pane and jumped down from the window to the second-floor porch. It was an easy jump. Benji managed it without even thinking about it. Once on the porch, he shook himself all over. It was his way of greeting the morning.

Benji wasn't very big, but he wasn't a very small dog, either. Looking at him, you'd have to call him a middle-sized mongrel. For *mongrel* was the word for Benji. He was of no breed that you could pin a name to, nor did he have a colour you could easily describe. Instead, his coat was of many colours, like Joseph's in the Old Testament – brown, and black, and a kind of rusty tan with a ruffle of white at his throat. But he wasn't entirely a homely dog, not Benji. His eyes were bright and his ears flopped playfully when he ran, as though they were running, too. His hair grew thick and would probably be soft and touchable, if anybody ever brushed it. But nobody ever did so it grew wild and tangled into a curly mat on his back and flanks.

His morning shake over, Benji trotted around the porch to the back of the house, where his 'staircase' would take him down into the morning.

Over the porch railing he jumped on to the roof of the house, trotting across the roof between the two gables. Here Benji stopped to look out over his domain, his private kingdom. From the height of his roof he could see the small, friendly town of Silver Creek. Benji's old house was just on the edge of the town. People didn't come out this way much, any more. Benji loved these early morning minutes alone on the roof; they made him feel like a king. He loved looking down across the farmyards on one side of the house. The cows were as small as children's toys and the chickens were only tiny dots moving around the henhouses. Silver Creek itself sparkled on the other side under a sky of blue like dolls' houses and play-stores, and the creek that gave the town its name wound like a shining ribbon between the farms and the city.

But breakfast was still calling, and Benji was hungry enough to answer. From the roof he jumped down lightly to the porch roof. He ran across to a con-necting arbour where the vines grew thickly now out of heavy trunks. Here he had to walk the tightrope of the narrow top rail of the arbour's trellis. He did it easily and without fear. The lattice work of the trellis was built in a stair-step pattern from top to bottom, and Benji followed these stairs down to a large heap of boxes, from which he jumped to the ground. Roofs, trellis, lattice, and boxes – these were Benji's 'staircase', and this was the way he was able to get up to the roof and out of the old, locked-up house. The hole in the second floor big bay window was his door.

As he moved happily down the worn path through the high grass, Benji felt good all over. This was going to be one fine day, filled with important things to do and important people to see. Even his coat itched with excitement. Ooops ... no, that was a flea. He sat down to scratch, and jumped up a minute later to chase a chicken. He meant it no harm, but chasing a chicken was part of this glorious morning, and Benji didn't want to miss a minute of it.

It took him half an hour to get to the heart of Silver Creek. It had been an adventurous thirty minutes.

He'd chased a rabbit through the tall grass, and investigated some very appetising smells that were coming out of a kitchen, but a large, black dog who lived there discouraged him from coming any closer to the source of the delicious aromas. Now he was trotting down the pavements of the little town, careful to cross with the light, watching the traffic both ways on every corner. Benji knew where he was going, and he wanted to get there in one piece.

The lawn on the courthouse square was emerald green and very lush, the grass kept perfectly, not a weed in sight. A large sign clearly ordered man and dog alike to 'Keep Off the Grass'. Benji ignored the sign, for the courthouse lawn was a short cut. He ambled across the grass, passing the sign without so much as a glance. Suddenly, a pair of official-looking legs appeared right in front of his little black nose.

'What's the matter? Can't you read?' asked the groundskeeper sternly. But there was a twinkle in his eye and he stooped to pat Benji on his shaggy head.

In reply, Benji licked the man's face, causing him to break into pleased laughter. But the dog couldn't stay for a visit today; he was late already.

Young Charlie Robbins was late this morning, too; he still had over two dozen papers to deliver. He tried to make up time by hurling them at the front steps of his customers' houses from the pavement. His twelve-year-old arm, made stronger by daily practice with a baseball, landed most of the papers neatly on the porches. But once in a while he'd miss, and then he'd grumble as he loped up to the front steps to tidy the paper and leave it where it belonged.

Charlie was just returning from the Steptoes' front door, having missed again, when he saw Benji coming towards him down the pavement. Boy and dog passed each other without a greeting, but a few seconds later, a rolled-up newspaper hurtled through the air over Benji's head. Without breaking stride, the dog leaped up and caught it in his mouth, careful not to tear it with his teeth. He looked at Charlie in triumph, as the newsboy gave him a freckled grin, and a thumbs-up sign.

The newspaper tucked neatly between his jaws, Benji trotted down the street and around the corner. He stopped before a clean white picket fence that ran all around the Chapman house, setting it off from the street and giving it privacy and dignity. The house itself was both expensive and beautiful, a two-storey Victorian home, white with green shutters and window trim. Around it grew many tall trees and brightly coloured flower beds. It was obviously the house of someone who had lots of money, although that hardly mattered to Benji.

Low to the ground, and almost invisible to human beings, was a small opening in the fence, a hole just Benji-size. Squeezing his sturdy body through the gap, Benji trotted over the grass and up the back steps to the kitchen door. He scratched at the screen door with his sharp nails. The marks on the door showed he had made this trip many times before.

'Morning, Benji. Come on in,' called a familiar voice.

Using his right front paw as a sharp little lever, Benji pried the kitchen door open and went into the house. The kitchen was warm, bright, and clean, filled with the morning sunshine. Good smells wafted on the air, and Benji tried to keep his mouth from watering, because he didn't want the newspaper, which he still carried in his jaws, to get wet.

'You're late this morning,' Mary remarked, cleaning up the breakfast dishes in her usual efficient way. 'You almost missed the kids. Here's your breakfast.' She set a delicious-smelling bowl on the floor and took the newspaper from him as she sank into a chair by the kitchen table. Mary was the Chapman housekeeper, a plump and motherly woman in her late forties. Plain spoken she was, and outspoken, too, but she had a heart as warm and big as her kitchen.

'What are the headlines?' she asked the dog as she turned to the paper. 'Who's done what to whom today?' Mary leaned her elbows on to the kitchen table, as Benji hungrily began to gulp down the food in his bowl.

The swinging door that led from the kitchen to the hall cracked open, and a nine-year-old head of ruffled hair poked through.

'Is Benji here yet?' The hair and the voice belonged to Paul Chapman, dressed for school and carrying his books.

'Yes, Benji's here yet,' Mary answered with a smile.

Paul turned and yelled back down the hall. 'Cindy! He's here!'

Mary frowned. 'He won't be for long if you don't stop that shouting,' she ordered. 'You know what happens if your father walks in.'

But Paul wasn't listening. Dropping his books on the table, he dashed across the roomy kitchen and knelt on the floor beside Benji, stroking the dog's coat. Benji licked the boy hello and stuck his nose back into the food bowl.

'I don't think Daddy understands about us and Benji,' Paul said sadly.

'I don't think you understand how much of an understatement you just made,' agreed Mary, turning a page of the paper.

'What does un-der-state-ment mean?'

'It means don't shout down the hall,' Mary laughed. She raised one eyebrow and nodded towards the door.

At that moment, Cindy Chapman burst in through the kitchen door, her ponytail bobbing with excitement. She too was dressed for school; her seven-year-old knees flashed beneath a fluffy pinafore.

'Where's Benji?' Cindy yelled.

'And don't shout in the kitchen!' Mary's voice rose in a loud whisper. 'Do you want your father in here?'

'No!' Cindy sounded desperate. 'But he's coming anyway! We've got to hide Benji!' Her pretty face was creased with worry.

'Phenomenal,' sighed Mary. It was some way to start the morning.

'Quick! He's right behind me!' Cindy's voice held tears of panic.

'We can put him outside!' Paul jumped up to carry out his idea.

'No!' Mary raised a hand to stop the boy. 'He's not through with his breakfast. He'd just stand there and scratch on the door.' She tried to think, tapping her cheek with her finger, glancing around the room for a solution to the problem. 'Uhhhh . . . give him to me. Put him in my lap.'

Paul and Cindy quickly dragged a reluctant Benji

away from his food and over to the table where Mary was sitting. She reached down and pulled him squirming into her lap.

'C'mon, boy. There you go,' she soothed. Benji, being somewhat larger than the average lapdog, didn't quite fit, even though Mary's lap was somewhat larger than the average lap. He sort of hung over on all sides, or *over*lapped. With an effort, Mary got him balanced. In a tone of warning, she advised him, 'Now stay balanced. It could mean your neck.'

Sliding her chair under the kitchen table, Mary made certain that her lap, and its contents, were hidden out of sight under the white tablecloth that hung halfway to the floor. She turned her attention to her coffee cup, adding sugar and cream from the bowl and jug on the table. Glancing down, she checked to see that Benji was staying put. Everything seemed quiet; the tablecloth wasn't stirring.

'There!' Mary breathed a heavy sigh of relief.

But all was not as she had supposed. There, sitting for all to see on the kitchen floor, was Benji's bowl, still half-filled with food.

'The bowl! Get the bowl!' Mary's voice was an urgent whisper.

As Paul dashed across the kitchen for the dish, a man's deep voice called from outside the kitchen door.

'Paul. Cindy.'

All heads turned to the hall door as Paul quickly straightened up and shoved the bowl behind his back. The three of them – Paul, Cindy, and Mary – froze in place, trying very hard to look as though they had not been caught doing anything. The kitchen door swung open and Dr Chapman put his head in.

'Come on, kids. It's time to go.' The head disappeared back into the hall as the door swung shut. But, before any of the culprits could move or relax, the door swung open a second time, and this time Dr Chapman came through it, a suspicious look forming on his handsome face.

'O.K. What's going on?' he demanded, in a tone of voice that meant no nonsense. He looked from one face to another, awaiting an answer.

'You heard your father, children. It's time to go,' offered Mary with a falsely wide smile. She glanced into her lap and gulped in surprise. Benji's tail was wagging out from under the tablecloth and on its way up into Dr Chapman's line of sight. With a hurried shove, she pushed the tail back under the snowy cloth, but the shove caught Benji off balance and he struggled to hold on to Mary's lap. As she felt Benji's nails digging in for a hold, Mary kept the false smile glued to her face, gritting her teeth behind it.

'Don't forget your books, Paul,' she called. 'Now, you kids run along. When your father says it's time to go, it's time to go.'

Cindy turned to her brother, who still clutched the food bowl in both hands behind his back. 'She's right, Paul. It *is* time to go.'

Smiling brightly, Paul edged over to the table, careful to keep his front turned towards his father and his hands out of sight. 'I guess so,' he conceded. 'Bye, Mary.' The boy leaned over to kiss the plump housekeeper on the cheek; as he did so, he managed to slide Benji's food bowl into her hands.

'Have a good day, Paul,' smiled Mary, frantically

shoving the bowl under the tablecloth. 'Good luck in your spelling test.'

Cindy bent to kiss Mary in her turn. 'Bye, Mary.' She saw the woman's eyes widen in something like horror, as she glanced towards her lap. Under the cloth and, mercifully, still invisible, Benji was struggling to get at the food bowl that kept him guilty company. His frantic turns made him slide right off Mary's lap. She hauled him back on, still keeping a grin fixed permanently on her jaws, which were beginning to ache with the strain.

'Bye-bye, honey. And don't forget we want you to look really pretty at your recital this afternoon. So don't you get that dress messy.'

'I won't,' called Cindy over her shoulder. 'C'mon, Dad, it's time to go.'

Cindy and Paul moved quickly to the kitchen door, one on each side of their father. The quicker they were out the door, the better it would be for all of them, especially for Benji.

But Dr Chapman gently put one large, strong hand on each of their heads, stopping them dead in their tracks. 'I believe I asked a question,' he stated firmly.

Paul peered up across his father's hand. 'Uh, what was that, Dad?' he asked innocently, his blue eyes open wide.

'What's been going on in here?' his father wanted to know.

'He's right, Paul,' Cindy said solemnly, stalling for time. 'I remember him asking that.'

'Now, come on, gang,' Dr Chapman's voice was warm, but stern. 'I know you're hiding something, so let's have it.' He looked closely at Mary, who still wore a smile that was too bright to be real. 'Starting with whatever you've got under the table, Mary.'

Mary's heart sank. She could see the kids glancing at each other, fear and worry in their looks. 'Yes, doctor,' she said quietly, and reached under the tablecloth. Slowly, very slowly, she drew out the food bowl and set it on the table. It was empty. The painted flowers on the bottom had a just-washed look.

Dr Chapman looked a little blank. 'What is that?'

'It's a bowl, doctor,' said Mary innocently. Under the tablecloth Benji began to move restlessly. Mary's other hand found his shaggy head and stroked it into quietness. 'An empty bowl.'

'I can see that, Mary.' The doctor frowned in impatience. 'What was in it?'

Mary hesitated. Then with a sigh she lowered her head. Her face wore a guilty expression.

'A snack.'

The doctor's frown deepened. 'Mary, how are we ever going to get the kids to eat a decent breakfast if they know they can come in here afterwards and get something they like better?' he complained.

'I never thought about it that way,' confessed Mary.

'Well, please do. No snacks after breakfast. O.K.?'

Mary looked Dr Chapman square in the eye. 'Yes, sir. You're absolutely right. No snacks.' She turned to Paul and Cindy, and stated firmly, 'I'm sorry, kids. There'll be no snacks after breakfast and that's final.'

Cindy tried hard to look disappointed. 'I guess we'll just have to grin and bear it,' she sighed.

'Sure gonna be hard to give up,' Paul agreed. But he couldn't smother the silly grin that almost covered his face.

'Get to school,' snapped Mary. 'Didn't you hear your father say it was time to go?'

Giggling, the kids ran out through the kitchen door, leaving their father to shake his head in wonderment and stare after them. Sometimes he just couldn't understand children! He turned to his housekeeper. 'We'll see you later, Mary.'

Mary listened carefully for a minute or two, to make certain they were all really gone. When she heard the car move out of the driveway, she heaved a sigh of relief, and slowly backed her chair out from under the table.

'Well, Benji . . . I think between the four of us we've got you another reprieve.'

She looked down into her lap and laughed. Benji was still clinging awkwardly to her knees, but his face was under the tablecloth. 'RRRRwooof,' he said in reply and the bark blew the tablecloth partially off his face, like an old man snoring under a newspaper. Mary lifted him out of her lap and set him gently on the floor.

'I'm glad too,' she said in response to his bark.

Benji shook himself and walked over to the screen door, sitting down in front of it with his back towards Mary. He could hear the water running and china rattling as she cleared the rest of the dishes off the table and began to wash them.

'It's a shame we have to go through this, 'cause he's really a pretty nice man. I mean overall. He's just a little stubborn on some things.' Mary glanced over her shoulder to see if Benji was listening. He wasn't. He sat firmly at the door, waiting for it to open and set him free.

'Oh, you're going to eat and run, huh?' Mary wiped her hands on her apron. 'One of these days I'm going to follow you just to see where you go,' she said. She stooped to ruffle his head. 'You know, you've got more independence than most *people*.'

Benji's tongue came out and he licked Mary's face. Laughing, she pushed him away.

'*And* more charm!' The housekeeper patted Benji on his rear and opened the screen door for him.

'Have a good day,' she called. 'We'll see you in the morning.'

Wagging his tail goodbye, Benji ran down the back steps and over the lawn. He was behind schedule, and he had to hurry.

TWO

Benji crouched down in the shrubbery, watching intently, never taking his eyes off her. Raising one white leg high, Mrs Finster's pedigreed Persian cat nibbled delicately on the fur near her foot. Benji's hair stood on end. That darn cat had been washing and grooming for an hour, it seemed like! Mrs Finster was watering some flowers in the corner of the yard. Keeping an eye on her, Benji dropped to his belly, and began to crawl around the shrubbery, circling the tree stump where the Finster cat sat preening, her back to Benji. Now he made a run for it.

Silently, Benji dashed across the Finster back yard and slid to a stop behind the brick barbecue pit. He peered out. Mrs Finster was still busy. The cat had switched her attention to her other leg, smoothing the white fur down with her rough tongue, a look of peaceful bliss on her small, round face. Benji dived under a bush for cover. Now he was directly behind her, stalking her slowly through the grass of the yard. Quietly, now, quietly. He came closer and closer.

Suddenly he shot up from the grass, barking furiously. With a screech of terror that would break windows, the Finster cat leaped wildly into the air, coming down with her just-washed fur sticking up in all directions. Yowling, she dashed towards the nearest tree, Benji barking hotly in pursuit. Frantically digging her claws deeply into the tree trunk, the cat scrambled up the tree and sat spitting and hissing on a branch. She peered furiously down at Benji, who stood barking below.

Mrs Finster whirled about, the watering can sloshing water as she waved it furiously at the dog. Her fat legs carried her across the grass with surprising speed.

'Stop it! You leave my Sweetie-Peetie alone, you primitive uncultured cur! I'm going to tell her to turn on you someday . . . and she'll do something dreadful! Then you'll be sorry!'

Benji ran for his life. Over his shoulder he could hear Mrs Finster still shouting at him. She was splashing water in all directions. 'You've got no decency!' she yelled.

Mrs Finster watched his brown and black form disappear around a corner at top speed. Then she turned to her darling, who was sulking in the tree.

'He's late today,' she remarked pleasantly.

Sweetie-Peetie miaowed in agreement.

Benji barked sharply to get Officer Tuttle's attention. The tall black man turned, and his handsome young face broke into a grin at the sight of the dog.

'Hello, Butch! Come here, boy!'

Benji took a running start across the grass and jumped into the policeman's arms.

'That's a good boy,' said Tuttle, patting him. The

officer put him down, reached into the pocket of his uniform, and drew out a small paper bag, screwed up into a ball. 'Look here,' he said. 'I saved you a little popcorn.' As they strolled along, he tossed pieces of the fluffy popcorn to Benji, who jumped and caught them in mid-air. Occasionally, Tuttle ate a few pieces himself. He enjoyed this daily treat.

The large park in front of the civic centre was part of Officer Tuttle's beat, the nicest part. Filled with grass and colourful flower-beds, it held many white stone benches, where older people and mothers with small children could sit and enjoy the sunshine on perfect days like this one. Benji and Tuttle moved side by side to a bench, where the officer sat down, easing his tired feet. Benji sat in front of him, his head cocked, one ear flopping, gulping popcorn, and listening to Tuttle's every word.

'There were some kids here earlier. They wanted to see you do some tricks.' Tuttle wondered briefly why Benji had been late. 'But I'm sure they'll be around some other day.' He bent to pick up a stick, showing it to Benji. 'Here,' he said. Then he threw it with all his might, high in the air and across the park. 'Go fetch it, Butch.'

With a bark of pleasure, Benji raced after the stick and pounced on it. Wagging his tail in triumph, he carried it proudly back to Officer Tuttle and laid it down at his feet. The officer patted his head and tossed him a piece of popcorn as a reward.

'That's a good boy,' he approved. 'Hey, guess what? Nancy and I set the date. In two months I'll be a married man.'

Benji looked up at him and woofed.

'Yeah, well, your day'll come.' He grinned down at the dog. 'Some cute little Pekinese'll come along and sweep you right off your feet.' Screwing up the empty popcorn pack, he patted the bench next to him. 'Climb up here and let me tell you about it.'

But Benji was behind schedule. He barked sharply, turned to go, then turned back and barked again in explanation.

Officer Tuttle shrugged. 'Suit yourself. I'll see you tomorrow, then.' As Benji trotted down the brick path the tall man called after him. 'Just remember when she gets you that I tried to give you a little advice.'

The town streets near the courthouse square and the civic centre were as busy and as bustling as Silver Creek ever was. Men and women moved across the avenue, on their way to work or to shop. Benji was careful to cross with the lights, as usual. He trotted around the corner on to Spruce Street and headed up town. A few doors from the corner stood Bill's Cafe. That was the name the well-worn, painted letters spelled out on the glass windows. Propped up against the cafe was a straight-back chair, and asleep in the chair was Bill himself, his glasses falling down over his nose. Benji came up to the chair and nuzzled his cold nose into the old man's hand.

Bill woke up with a start, trying to clear the cobwebs from his sleepy brain. Then, pushing his glasses back up his nose, he saw Benji.

'Oh, hello, Sam,' the old man said, his kindly face breaking into a smile. He squinted at the sun, then took an ancient gold pocket watch out of his waistcoat and checked the time. 'Hey, where've you been?' Bill demanded. 'You let me sleep too long. I ought to be in there gettin' ready for the rush.' Both Bill and Benji knew there wouldn't be any rush, just a handful of regular customers, but both of them loved this game and played it faithfully. 'Today's the homemade stew special and you know how long that takes.'

'Wooof,' said Benji.

Old Bill chuckled. 'You and Margaret,' he said to the dog. 'She used to say, "Bill, the whole world ain't going to come to an end if you miss the rush one day." ' Blue eyes twinkled over rimless glasses. 'But, just in case she was wrong, I'd better get moving.'

With an effort, the old man climbed out of the chair in which he'd been dozing. 'I'll get your pay,' he told Benji. 'It's just inside.' He stepped into the cafe and returned a minute later with a meaty bone. 'There you go,' he said, stooping to pat the dog, and handing him the bone.

Benji woofed his thanks as best he could with his mouth full of bone, and trotted off back down Spruce Street.

'You're welcome,' old Bill called after him, waving a hand. 'And be on time tomorrow! It's meat loaf day!'

Silver Creek was a prosperous town that boasted several handsome parks, but two of them were Benji's personal favourites. The large civic centre park near the courthouse, because that's where Officer Tuttle fed him popcorn and put him through his paces, and this pretty little park, that seemed to be 'for looks only'. There were no old people on the benches here, or children playing, just neatly cut grass and trimmed shrubbery, and flower-beds that were well-weeded and well-cared for. What Benji liked so much about this little park was 'his' litter basket, his very own property. He checked it daily.

Today, as always, he jumped on to the empty bench nearest the basket and tugged with his foot until the basket tilted over, the top resting against the bench. Now Benji was able to rummage around conveniently, and he spent a few happy minutes nosing in it. But there was nothing there this morning to interest him – a few scraps, but nothing wonderful to a dog with a belly full of breakfast and popcorn, a dog with a meaty bone for his dinner. So he jumped off the bench, letting the litter basket right itself again, picked up his precious bone, and headed for home.

Ferdo was out, lying asleep across the pavement ... sixty pounds of mean and muscular dog. He was the neighbourhood bully.

Benji trotted closer.

Ferdo felt vibrations. His eyes opened, and his head shot up, his large brown eyes focusing on the bone in Benji's mouth. A low, mean rumble started deep in his throat.

Benji trotted still closer, never breaking his stride.

That bone looked mighty good, and was getting nearer all the time. Ferdo licked his chops and turned a withering look on Benji – a look guaranteed to freeze the bravest heart. The growl was a definite noise now, building in loudness until it thundered into the morning air as a series of resounding barks. Ferdo sprang forward, snapping and yapping. But he was caught up short by the chain that tied him fast to a tree.

Without ducking his head, Benji trotted jauntily

27

right under the chin of the huge dog, and bounced down the block. A smile seemed to spread across his face.

Ferdo's ferocious roar turned into a whimpering yelp. His ears drooped as low as his spirit as he watched Benji dancing off through the dappled sunlight. With a sigh, he dropped his large head on to his paws and stretched out on the pavement again. It wasn't going to be such an interesting day after all, he decided.

This was the time of day that Benji loved the best – his rounds over, the going home time. Benji enjoyed most the feeling of independence that his wanderings gave him. He loved his friendships with old Bill and Officer Tuttle, he loved being 'Sam' and 'Butch', earning his bones and doing tricks for popcorn. Best of them all, he loved Cindy and Paul and Mary; he loved them so much that he even thought of himself always as 'Benji', the name they'd given him. If he didn't have a home of his own, if he didn't value so highly the freedom his roving nature seemed to demand, why, he could imagine sleeping across the foot of Paul's bed one night, and Cindy's the next. He could imagine Mary's warm lap on a full-time basis. But he always put these thoughts out of his furry head. Because, although nobody owned him, Benji *did* have a home, and best of all he liked the going home time.

The old Powell house stood on the edge of town, just before Silver Creek gave way to farmland. Nobody had lived in the place for more than forty years. Once an impressive mansion built by a rich family, it now stood in partial decay, turning grey outside for lack of paint, its bushes and its shrubs grown to the height of trees, shrouding the old home in shadows. The glass in several of the windows had been broken out, and a shutter hung down from its hinges like one of Benji's floppy ears.

Even in the bright sunshine there was something creepy about the old place, and hardly anybody went near it any more. No one had been inside since it was closed up. There were rumours that it was haunted, that old Mr Powell had done something terrible there to old Mrs Powell, and kids would cross the street to avoid going past the house. But Benji didn't mind. He loved the old place; he loved its privacy and its quiet. Besides, nobody knew he was living there, and he had it all to himself.

The bone clenched in his teeth like a flag, Benji turned into the back yard of the abandoned house. He climbed up the stair-stepping arbour on the way to the broken bay window. Over the boxes and up the lattice work of the arbour, across the roof between the gables, over the porch railing, through the broken window. Benji was home.

He padded through the shadows of the musty upstairs bedroom. The house was dark, even though the day was bright outside. All the old lace and velvet curtains, heavy with ancient dust, had been pulled across the windows years ago; they moved slightly as the wind pushed through the broken glass. Cobwebs stretched their way across many of the doorways, and hung from the ceiling and the branches of the chandeliers. The only light in the house peeked in from the holes and tears in the drapes; scattered patches of sunlight lay like bright little rugs here and there on the old carpets. Most of the furniture was shrouded in large, grey sheets, giving a lumpy, ghostly look to the rooms, but here and there heavy Victorian pieces still reflected, through thick layers of dust, the splendour the old house once knew.

Benji moved through the shadows and pattered across the hall and down the winding stairs. A miniature painting had fallen from its nail and was lying on one of the steps; Benji walked carefully around it. The staircase ended in a wide downstairs foyer that led from the front door to the spacious parlours. Here, under the heavy cloth covering the hall table, Benji had made himself a very comfortable home. From various parts of the house at various times he had 'rescued' a blanket, a couple of towels and even a pillow, which he'd dragged in to sleep on in style. It was more like a nest than a home, but to Benji it was everything. Now, his long day almost over, he settled down on the pillow to work on his bone, utterly content.

Suddenly there was a sound at the front door, a noise that Benji had never heard before. A rasping, scraping sound that made the fur along his spine stand on end.

THREE

Benji froze, and the bone dropped from his paws. There it was again, that sound he couldn't identify. Every nerve in the dog's body was tingling now, and his ears stood to attention, while his little black nose twitched, sniffing the air. He moved out of his box cautiously, and took up a position behind a large piece of draped furniture. There he could keep an eye on the front door without being seen.

But everything seemed quiet. The scraping had stopped. Evidently the key wouldn't work. Benji turned to go back to his bone, when another, louder sound made his neck-fur prickle. It was the sound of sawing, metal on metal, that harsh, grating sound that sets a dog's teeth on edge. Immediately, he scooted back to his vantage point, crouching down with eyes fixed on the door. The sawing sound continued, and Benji crept forward across the room until he came to the corner of the foyer. There, he crouched down again, peering around the corner at the front door.

He could dimly make out the thin blade of a hacksaw, coming through the door frame, sawing back and forth across the old, rusted lock. Benji looked closer. Through the torn shade of the foyer window, he could glimpse three figures on the front porch outside. One, a thin man in his twenties, was working the hacksaw blade back and forth. Looking over his shoulder was a muscular boy of about the same age, carrying what appeared to be two heavy grocery sacks. The third shadowy figure was that of a girl, and Benji thought that she was probably very pretty. At least from what little he could see.

'I thought you said you could pick it!' Henry Newton's worried whisper carried to Benji's keen ears.

'It didn't work,' Riley Bonner whispered back loudly. 'But this will.'

'Yeah, but how're we goin' to lock it when we get inside?' Henry wanted to know.

'Why lock it?' demanded Riley. 'Nobody in their right mind wants *in* this place. And I may want *out* in a hurry.'

'Can't you go any faster?' Linda Fulmer complained. 'Somebody's going to see us!'

At that moment the blade lurched through the lock with a final rasp, and the hacksaw pulled free.

'Done,' said Riley.

'Try it,' breathed Henry.

Benji watched the doorknob turn and the door creak slowly open; he turned like a shot and scampered back to the safety of the corner. As the door swung open fully, Riley, Henry, and Linda crowded in the doorway, peering inside, trying to see into the gloom. Riley stood smack in the centre; his face showed both doubt and suspicion. Linda, standing to one side, peeked around Riley's bony shoulder. Next to her, Henry tried to balance two heavy brown bags.

'Well, go on in,' Henry urged Riley.

But Riley didn't budge. 'This was your idea. You go first,' he retorted stubbornly. He was trying to swat a cobweb which had drifted across his face.

'I can't,' said Henry with a sigh.

'How come?'

'You're standing in the doorway,' Henry pointed out.

'For pity's sakes!' Linda snapped impatiently. '*I'll* go first.' She didn't want them to be seen. She brushed by Riley, nudging him to one side, and Henry followed her into the gloomy foyer. Benji's guess had been right; Linda *was* very pretty. He pulled back from around the corner, wondering what he should do, and scurried to his 'nest'. For the moment, watchful waiting seemed to be the safest plan. From beneath the tablecloth Benji's bright eyes gleamed out at the trio of strangers.

Henry's eyes had adjusted to the gloom, and he was staring around the vast foyer with its faded elegance. 'Hey ... wow ... this is really something!' he whistled.

'You've got weird taste, Henry.' Riley shook his head.

As the door clicked shut behind the three young people, the light coming into the foyer dimmed again. The trio blinked, then separated to move cautiously across the foyer and peer into the huge parlour. Henry put the sacks of groceries down on the floor close by Benji's nest, while Linda rubbed her finger across the dust on a mahogany sideboard.

'It's hard to believe that nobody's lived here for over forty years,' she breathed.

'Except old man Powell and his lovely wife's head,' retorted Riley.

'Leave the haunted house stuff to the kids, O.K.?' frowned Linda.

Riley shrugged. 'I was just joking.' He glanced around with a touch of fear. 'I hope.' But he was convinced things were moving in the shadows.

Henry had undraped a delicate French loveseat covered in blue silk, and was sinking down into it. 'Hey,' he called, 'this chair is great.'

'This whole place is great,' agreed Linda. 'It's really perfect.' She moved off to the sitting room, a vast parlour with faded murals on the walls, and a glittering chandelier hanging from the ceiling. 'I think Mitch will like it a lot,' she called back over her shoulder. 'This room looks comfortable. You can set up in here.'

Henry wasn't listening. Always hungry, he was fumbling around in one of the grocery sacks for something to eat. At last he found what he wanted and brought out a pudding cup, a little single portion of dessert in a can. From his hiding place, Benji looked eagerly. He was always hungry too. He watched Henry pull the tab on the cup, and peel off the lid. Benji blinked in surprise. He'd never seen anything quite like it before.

'I don't know, Linda Sue,' came Riley's voice from the next room. 'It seems like we're right under the whole town's noses.'

Linda's voice replied with a touch of anger. 'I told you not to call me Linda Sue any more. It's just Linda. And especially don't call me that in front of Mitch!'

'I'm sorry, I'm sorry.'

Linda knew she had been harsh. Riley didn't know

how she felt about Mitch. 'As long as we're careful, we can come and go through the back with almost no chance of being seen,' she said.

Henry pulled a plastic spoon out of the grocery bag and dipped it into the pudding cup. Benji's eyes never left the pudding cup. 'At least it's got a roof on it and that beats being out in the woods somewhere with the bugs,' Henry offered, spooning pudding into his wide mouth.

'If it's all the same,' Riley called back, 'I'll take the bugs.'

'Well . . . I think Mitch will like it. And he'll make the final decision.' Linda took a last look around, then said with approval, 'I'm glad you thought of it, Henry. Come on, let's go.'

She headed for the door. Henry took another hasty bite of pudding and followed her, leaving the half-full cup on the chair near where he'd been sitting. Riley fell in behind the other two. He didn't look very happy.

'Just for the record, I'm not glad you thought of it, Henry. This place gives me the screaming creeps.'

The door slammed shut behind them. A cloud of dust swirled up from the old rug.

Benji listened for a minute, then looked out to make certain they were gone. When satisfied that he was once more alone, he got up and made his way to the sacks of groceries. Long experience had taught him that bags often contained good things to eat. He sniffed at each sack, one at a time, then checked out the contents of both, dumping over one of the bags in the process. No luck. Everything was tucked into cans, bottles, and boxes.

Then Benji jumped on to Henry's chair and tried the pudding cup. His tongue came out for a tentative lick and his whiskers trembled with happiness. Delicious! Benji dearly loved desserts and rarely had a chance at them. Picking the pudding cup up in his teeth, he carried it to his nest and settled down on his pillow. He steadied the can between his front paws and began to polish it off. He was enjoying the unexpected feast, and had already forgotten the intruders, the strangers who had forced their way into his house.

FOUR

'He doesn't look like his feelings are hurt to me,' said Mary.

'Well, they are,' replied Cindy. 'I can tell. He's just too polite to say.' Cindy, Paul, and Mary looked down at Benji, whose whiskers were deep into his food bowl. If gulping down table scraps meant that one's feelings were hurt, then Benji was injured indeed, because he didn't stop swallowing long enough to even blink at the conversation.

Mary unrolled her newspaper and settled back against the porch step to read it. 'I'm sure he doesn't mind where he eats, as long as he eats,' was her opinion.

'But he's always eaten *inside* with us,' Paul protested, looking around the Chapman back porch with disgust.

'I'm sorry, kids.' Mary shook her head. 'Yesterday scared me out of ten years' growth.' She looked at the two of them sharply over the top of her newspaper. 'Do you realise what would've happened if your father had found him under that table?' She gave a little shiver, remembering a lapful of trouble.

'He'd've fainted,' giggled Cindy.

'He'd've fired me on the spot,' said Mary.

Paul shot Mary an oh-come-on look. 'He'd never fire *you*,' he said.

'If he did, he'd have to fire us too,' stated Cindy firmly, her chin in the air.

'That's nice,' replied Mary dryly without looking up from her newspaper, 'but it's a bit impractical.'

'What does im-prac-ti-cal mean?' asked Paul.

Mary waved her chubby arm around at the back porch. 'It means this is the best solution to the problem for right now. So don't let's talk about it any more, O.K.?' She rustled the newspaper to emphasise that the subject was closed.

Cindy slumped down with a sigh and wistfully rubbed Benji's head. Then, after a minute of unbroken silence, she asked, 'Couldn't we explain to Daddy and make him understand about Benji?'

Mary shook her head kindly, an expression of understanding crossing her merry face. 'Honey, to your father, Benji is just a stray,' she said gently.

'But he's not!' Cindy cried. Then she saw Mary's look, and she, too, glanced down at Benji. It would be had to imagine more of a stray than the mongrel on the porch right now. 'I mean, not really,' she added. Then Cindy's loyalty flared up again. 'And even if he is, what's wrong with that?' she wanted to know.

'Just because Uncle Chris got bit one time,' put in Paul.

'Your Uncle Chris almost died that one time,' Mary reminded them.

'But this is different!' Cindy protested.

'Yes,' chimed in Paul. 'Dad says we shouldn't think all teachers are bad just because we don't like Miss Gildy, so why does he think all dogs are bad just because one bit Uncle Chris?'

Mary peered over the newspaper, glanced from one young face to the other. Kids asked the darndest questions? She put down the paper, biting her lip.

'Kids ... if he thought it was best for you, your father would give you the shirt off his back ...' she began, then gasped in horror as a sudden thought hit her. 'His shirt! Oh, I forgot to iron his shirt!'

Scrambling clumsily to her feet, she picked up Benji's empty food bowl and started for the kitchen in a hurry. Dr Chapman would raise the roof if his shirt wasn't ready when he wanted it. As she opened the door, she called over her shoulder, 'Don't stay out here too long!' The screen door slammed behind her.

'We won't,' promised Cindy.

Brother and sister waited in silence, listening to Mary's footsteps hurry through the kitchen and out again on her way to the laundry room. Then, with a glance at Paul, Cindy eased herself up quietly to look through the screen door.

'Is she gone?' whispered Paul.

'Yes,' Cindy whispered back. 'Let's do our plan.'

'O.K. I'll hold Benji if you go and get it.'

'O.K.' Cindy tiptoed in the back door, and on up to her room to get 'it'.

'It' was a special dog brush, and Benji was in sore need of it. His coat had been neglected for so long it looked like something no self-respecting cat would drag in. Grooming him was no easy matter as Paul and Cindy found out. After fifteen solid minutes of brush-

39

ing, with Benji squirming and Cindy holding him, Paul had barely made a dent in the mess.

'Hurry up,' urged Cindy. 'We've got a whole side to go and she'll be back any minute.'

'I'm going as fast as I can,' answered Paul, beads of sweat on his upper lip like a little moustache. 'You want it to look good, don't you?'

'Of course, silly, but I want *my* side to look good, too.'

'We may not get to your side today,' her brother said. 'He's got terrible tangles.'

Cindy pulled Benji's face around and looked into his eyes. 'Benji! What *have* you been into?' Benji just yawned.

'I think it was a fight with a giant wad of chewing gum,' said Paul, brushing his hair off his damp forehead.

'O.K., kids.' Mary's voice came to them from the kitchen. 'You better get on up front before your father comes back here looking for you.'

By the time she had reached the kitchen door and was looking at them through the screen, both kids had scooted around in front of Benji, hiding as much of him as they could.

'What is this?' demanded Mary, instantly suspicious.

'Close your eyes,' said Paul.

Mary gave him one of her looks, eyes narrow, mouth set. 'Now that's very clever. I catch you up to something. I close my eyes. And you get rid of the evidence, right?'

Paul shook his head, a grin tugging at his lips. 'We're not doing anything wrong. We just want to show you something.'

'Please close your eyes,' Cindy begged.

Mary rolled her eyes up to heaven with a face that clearly asked 'Why am I such a sucker?' Then she grinned back. 'O.K., but hurry.' She closed her eyes.

At once, Paul and Cindy began to 'arrange' Benji, turning the dog this way and that to show off his best angle.

'Turn him round,' whispered Cindy urgently. 'He's wrong side out.'

'I know. I know.' Paul pulled at Benji, who was getting tired of being patient. Benji dug his nails into the porch step and refused to budge.

It took the efforts of both of them to turn him round; 'Come on, Benji,' they pleaded and urged until, at last, he was facing 'right side out'.

'Now stand right there,' whispered Paul, giving him a few final strokes with the brush.

'O.K., Mary,' called Cindy.

Mary opened her eyes and looked down at Benji and the two children kneeling beside him. She looked hard, but she was not at all sure what she was supposed to be seeing. Benji was no show dog – that was for sure. The side that was showing looked better, but not by much, and Mary was no expert.

'What do you think?' asked Paul proudly.

'Uhhhh ... I think you're going to have to give me a hint,' Mary shrugged, coming out on the step for a closer look.

Paul's face fell, and Cindy's lower lip started to tremble. 'You mean you can't even tell the difference?' Cindy wailed.

'You've got to!' urged Paul. 'It's important! Look.'

He spoke into Benji's ear. 'Turn round, Benji. Come on.' Benji didn't move, and sister and brother pushed and tugged until he was turned round.

'This is *before*,' explained Paul. Then he managed to turn the dog back again. 'And this is *after*.'

The light dawned on Mary. Now she saw the difference. A small difference, but a difference. 'Oh ... you brushed him out. Sure.' She stooped down to inspect their work. 'You should have shown me *before* before you showed me *after*.' She examined Benji on both sides. 'He looks very nice,' she said critically. 'On *this* side.'

'We didn't have time to finish my side,' explained Cindy.

'Does it make him *not* look like a stray?' asked Paul hopefully.

Mary pursed her lips in thought. 'Well, I never really ...' Then it hit her fully, the reason they had worked so hard and were caring so much. 'Ohhhh ... now I see!' she exclaimed. 'This is all for your father's benefit, isn't it?'

'We figured if we made him look real nice then Daddy would like him,' said Paul eagerly.

Mary sighed deeply, and sat down on the steps. She patted Benji without thinking, as she tried to find the right words for Paul and Cindy. 'I'm afraid,' she began slowly, 'that the problem is a bit more complicated than just making him look nice.'

'It'll help, won't it?' interrupted Cindy.

'Well ...' Mary sighed again. She smoothed her apron.

'What else do we have to do?' Paul asked.

'Daddy *is* wrong, isn't he?' Cindy added.

42

Mary held up a protesting hand. 'Now, Cindy, I never . . .'

This time it was Paul who interrupted. 'We *have* to be right 'cause you're on our side.'

'And you always say right wins over wrong,' Cindy said quickly.

'Oh, boy,' Mary said softly to heaven. It was more complicated than she'd thought.

'Paul! Cindy! Let's go!' called Dr Chapman from inside the house.

A quick look of relief appeared on Mary's face. Saved by the bell. 'We'll finish this another time,' she said briskly. 'Now you'd better get up there before he gets back here or there may not *be* another time. Go on. Scoot!'

Cindy and Paul were already hurrying inside. The threat of 'no Benji next time' was enough to scare them properly.

'See you later,' called Paul. ''Bye.' He banged through the door.

Cindy reached the door and turned back. 'Oh, here, Mary.' She handed the housekeeper the dog brush. 'You wouldn't let him spend his whole day half-and-half, would you?' she coaxed. Then she disappeared inside.

Mary sighed and turned to Benji, who stood looking at her with large, brown, warm, sad eyes. 'Sometimes I wonder who's in charge here. Me or them?' she asked.

Benji barked. To Mary, it sounded like 'them'.

The Finster cat yowled in fright and made a lightning dash for her tree, with Benji, barking loudly, right on her tail. The back door slammed open, and Mrs Finster came shrieking across the back yard at the double.

'Get away from her, you commonplace savage!' She flapped her apron at him.

Benji turned tail and headed out, fast.

'You uncivilised ruffian!' Mrs Finster shouted after him. 'Sweetie-Peetie's going to get you one day and I'm going to let her because you're nothing but a barbarian!' The old lady shook her fist at the dog's tail as it vanished around the next corner. 'And you're not nice!'

Mrs Finster looked up at her white cat, perched on the tree limb.

'He looks like he's just been brushed,' she remarked, puzzled.

Sweetie-Peetie miaowed in agreement.

'Well, I can see that you've given some thought to our little talk yesterday,' said Officer Tuttle, throwing Benji a piece of popcorn. 'Got yourself all dolly-dooed up and slicked down.'

'RRRRRwoof!' denied Benji, sitting up and begging for some more popcorn.

'Don't tell me,' said Officer Tuttle, smiling. 'I know when a guy's out looking. When you find one you like, you bring her by here and we'll go through some of your paces.' He motioned for Benji to roll over, and Benji obliged. 'We'll show her how smart you are. That'll impress her.'

Benji came up from the roll with grass on his back. Officer Tuttle frowned and leaned down from the bench on which he was sitting. 'Now look what we've done,' he said. 'Got you all messed up. We can't have that, can we?' His strong hand gently brushed the grass from Benji's coat. Benji pushed his black nose up against the popcorn bag for more, woofing softly. Turning it upside down, the policeman showed him that it was empty.

'No. It's all gone. See? Besides,' he grinned, 'I think you ought to get on with the search. Some lovely young thing's out there just waiting for you.'

Bill came out of a sound sleep when the cold, wet nose pushed into his hand. Waking with a half-finished snore, he yawned and stretched his stiff old arms, then shoved the glasses back up his nose.

'Oh ... hi, Sam.' The old man checked his pocket watch and yawned again. 'You better start looking for another client for yourself,' he said seriously to the dog. 'I made a big decision last night. Decided I've worried about this place too long. So I'm goin' to shut 'er down.'

Benji barked in surprise.

'Well ...' the old man shrugged in answer to the bark, 'I haven't decided *when* yet. Got to take these big decisions one at a time. I figure it'll be a week or two till I make the decision.'

Bill pulled his aching limbs out of the chair and moved slowly to the refrigerator to get Benji's bone. 'Probably be next year or the year after when I close 'er up. Don't want to rush into anything.' He handed Benji the bone, a really fine one, with thick shreds of meat on it. 'Here you go.'

Benji woofed his thanks, wagging his tail in appreciation. Then he took the bone in his mouth and headed on down the road.

'You're welcome,' called Bill. 'Say! You look different this morning. Did you fall in a lake or something?' He scratched his head and watched the little dog dodging the feet of the shoppers hurrying by.

His dinner earned, Benji set off for the next stop on his daily rounds. He had no idea as he trotted down the street that he was trotting towards his destiny, towards the beginning of a great and wonderful – and perilous – adventure.

FIVE

Benji came to a sudden halt, unable to believe his own eyes. That was *his* litter basket, his own personal property. Only *he* knew the trick of tilting it over on its side to get at the goodies inside. Who was this *other* dog rummaging through Benji's own litter basket, this dirty little white dog with matted fur? She hadn't seen him yet. Benji dropped his bone behind a bush for safekeeping, nudged it carefully out of sight, and moved towards the dog and the basket.

Apparently she was starving, because she was going after a bread crust that Benji wouldn't even wipe his feet on. She still hadn't noticed him. Benji felt a strange stirring inside, but he took it to be sympathy for her hunger. He watched her in silence for a minute, then woofed in a friendly manner.

The little white dog looked up, startled, from her half-chewed bread crust. Her upper lip drew back, exposing her teeth in a snarl. She forced a growl from her small throat. Benji persisted – he wanted to be friends. Once again he woofed, adding a tail-wag and a little sneeze to show his good intentions and his playfulness. But she continued to snarl and growl, and now she barked twice. They were not friendly barks.

Inching a little closer, Benji continued to wag and woof. The little dog made a short dart forward and snapped at him with her teeth, missing his ear by inches. She was definitely *not* feeling friendly. Benji dropped to the ground, woofing gently, and inched forward on his belly. He was puzzled at her actions – and his. Now, Benji didn't hate anybody in the world, not even the Finster Persian cat; it wasn't in his nature to hate. But it wasn't in his nature to try *this* hard to make friends with a dog who made it so very clear that she didn't want to play. So why was he taking all this trouble? He couldn't figure it out. All he knew was that we wanted to play with her, that he felt so very sorry for her, alone and dirty and hungry.

Hungry! Benji glanced over his shoulder to the shrubbery, where that meaty bone lay hidden. The other dog snapped again, snarling, and fell to chewing at the bread crust. Uttering a sharp bark, Benji ran to the shrubbery and pulled out the bone, dragging it over in her direction.

The little dog's eyes widened at the sight of the juicy morsel in Benji's mouth. Benji knew he had caught her interest – or at least the bone had. Benji moved a couple of cautious inches closer. She snarled again, but it was a light snarl, not as hostile as before. She kept her eyes glued to that bone.

Dropping the bone on the grass, Benji began to nudge it towards her with his nose. She stood as still as a statue, watching that feast come towards her on the grass. She hadn't eaten in days; she couldn't help lick-ing her chops, and Benji knew he'd broken through. He pushed the bone closer. The little dog took one step forward, then another. Benji lay down on the grass, his head next to the bone, watching her.

Her small, delicate head stretched out towards the bone; Benji lay still, not moving a muscle. She licked the bone – once, then again – and, with a gentleness that flooded Benji's heart with bliss, she licked his nose. Oh, how soft and tender that nose-lick! Benji's bones seemed to melt; he had never felt this way before. How beautiful the day suddenly became, he thought, as he watched her greedily nibbling the bone.

He didn't regret a single bite. Everything she did seemed to him to be more graceful than anything he'd seen before. When she had satisfied her hunger, Benji felt that now was the time for him to carry out a plan he had been forming.

He got up and trotted away, barking over his shoulder for her to follow. Nervous and unsure of herself in this new situation, she trotted behind for a few steps, the bone in her mouth, then stopped, then started again, following Benji out of the park.

Benji led her across streets and through alleyways, always checking back to make certain that she was behind him. Sometimes she appeared confused by the traffic, and by the people who filled the streets of the little town. But Benji, barking, always urged her on, and she always followed ... until, tired and hot, she crawled into the cool shade under a ramp in an alley and lay down, panting with heat and exhaustion.

Benji turned and barked for her to get up again and follow. She barked no. She really was very tired and had no idea how much further they had to go. No wonder she wouldn't get up! Benji came back to her, picked up the bone so she wouldn't have to carry it, and, woofing gently, he assured her that it wasn't much further. He started down the alley and turned again, woofing instead of barking. With a little sigh, she pulled herself up and began to follow.

It was only a few more blocks before Benji stopped in front of the hole in the fence around the Chapman house. She stopped too, uncertain. She looked up at the huge house; the size of everything amazed her. She watched as Benji wriggled through the broken pickets, but she wasn't sure she wanted to follow. She stopped and blinked behind the white furry fringe that covered her eyes.

Benji's shaggy head poked back through the opening. He dropped the bone and barked at her sharply. She didn't budge. So he squeezed back through the fence. Nuzzling and woofing, he circled round her, urging her forward. She didn't budge. He backed off and woofed again, a note of urgency in his voice. Finally she made up her mind. She had trusted him this far. She got to her feet, and trotted after him through the fence and into the Chapman yard. Benji ducked back through the hole, retrieved the bone and led the way up to the kitchen door.

'Benji?! Is that you?' Mary couldn't believe her ears. Benji scratching at the door when the children were at school?

But the answering woof could not be mistaken.

'What in the world are you doing here at this time of day?' she demanded, coming to the screen door and pushing it open. Her eyes opened wide at the sight of the little white dog. 'Well, what have we here?' she exclaimed.

Benji seemed to grin, wagging his tail like a flag. Mary grinned back.

'I do believe you've found yourself a girlfriend.'

Benji nuzzled the little dog's ear fondly. It was plain that he agreed with Mary, and wasn't ashamed of it.

Mary put her hands on her ample hips and pretended to frown. 'A fine thing! I risk my neck feeding you breakfast every morning and what do you do? Go out and find another woman!'

Benji woofed sheepishly, his grin becoming silly around the whiskers.

'Well . . .' Mary smiled, 'I guess there's no hard feelings.' She stooped down and petted the little white dog on her grimy head. 'You look like you need a good meal and a good brushing. And I just happen to have the materials for both.' She cocked one eye at Benji, who cocked one ear back. 'And don't you sit there so smug-looking as if you didn't plan it that way!'

Benji replied with a playful sneeze.

'Oh, sure,' said Mary. 'You'd better watch out for him,' she warned the little white dog. 'He's a sneak.'

Mary stood up. 'I'll be back in a minute,' she said.

And she was, with a bowl of delicious scraps and Benji's brush. It took half an hour to get the little white dog clean and fluffy; she had not been groomed in weeks. Now, fed and brushed, she sat on the steps next to Benji.

Mary gave a low whistle of admiration, and Benji just stared. This was the prettiest, most attractive little dog either one of them had ever seen. Her fur, brushed to a radiant fluffiness, was like snowy whipped cream; her little topknot framed a face of such beauty that it took Benji's breath away. It was evident to both of them that this little dog had class. She was no stray; she was a pedigree if either one of them had ever seen a pedigree. Had she been dognapped? Was she a runaway? She had probably just strayed off her home territory and got lost.

All Benji knew was that his heart was lost completely. She was gorgeous beyond his wildest dreams. His heart beat faster with love and pride. He wanted to do every trick he knew just for her; he wanted to give her the meatiest, juiciest bones in all the world.

'Well, Benji,' said Mary at last, 'all I've got to say is that you've got a mighty high-faluting-looking girl-friend there.' She leaned over close to Benji and whispered into his ear. 'You're not in over your head, are you?'

Benji licked her on the nose. 'Dumb question.' Mary laughed. She turned to the little girl dog. 'Well, I guess if you're going to be a regular we ought to think of something to call you.' She put her hand gently under the little dog's chin and pulled her pretty face around so that she could look deeply into it. She shook her head. 'But I don't know what it will be.' Mary waved in Benji's direction. 'Now *he* was easy. He just looks like a Benji. But I'm afraid you look like Park Avenue and I'm just not too up on high-class names.'

Mary gazed off into the distance for inspiration, and a dreamy smile played over her lips as she remembered something. 'The closest I ever came to Park Avenue was when George used to tell me that some day he was going to make enough money to take me to Tiffany's and buy me anything I wanted.' Her face grew soft and dim as she gave herself up to the beloved memory.

Then suddenly she smiled. 'Hey, we could call you Tiffany. To me, that's about as high class as you can get.' She looked sharply at Benji for his approval, and Benji woofed, his tail wagging with pleasure.

'Then Tiffany it is,' Mary said. She stood up, brushing some of Tiffany's hair off her lap. 'Now you two be on your way,' she ordered. 'I'm one feeding and a brushing behind in my chores.'

Benji jumped to his feet and trotted lightly down the porch steps, expecting Tiffany to follow, but Tiffany just sat there, gazing at Mary. The little dog's memories had been stirred, memories of good food eaten from a bowl, not a garbage can, memories of soft, gentle hands brushing and grooming her coat, of a woman's voice and a comfortable lap. Freedom meant very little to Tiffany; she had been a pampered pet, a cuddly lapdog. She looked from Mary to Benji back to Mary again, while Benji waited at the foot of the steps, fear building in his heart.

Mary understood.

'Life's just full of decisions, isn't it?' she said softly to Tiffany.

Tiffany looked back to Benji again, and her decision was made. She scampered down the steps to his side. Both of them looked up at Mary. Benji felt his spirit soaring to the skies; he had never been happier in his life. He barked once, echoed by a lighter bark from Tiffany.

'You're welcome,' Mary replied. 'And have a good

day.' She watched them turn and run off together, the shaggy mongrel and the beautiful little pedigree. Something suspiciously like a tear formed in her eye, but she blinked it back. As she turned to go into the house, Mary noticed something on the porch. She bent to pick it up. 'Hey,' she yelled after them, waving the bone, 'You forgot . . .' But they were gone. Shaking her head, Mary smiled warmly, and then went back into the kitchen.

Tiffany lay in the soft grass of the park. A fragment of sunlight found its way through the leafy trees and lighted her newly brushed silky fur, forming a pretty halo around her face. Benji sat nearby – just watching her. He couldn't remember ever having been so happy and excited and . . . well . . . so *glad* the sun was out and the fat bees were flitting through the air among the flowers. It was a glorious day!

With a playful bark, he bounced up and ran joyously around her in a series of dizzying circles, yapping constantly. Then he stopped quickly and softly nuzzled Tiffany's ear.

Tiffany turned her head and looked at him shyly – then briskly bounded away across the grass and through a hole in the shrubbery.

The chase was on! Benji went scampering after, dodging around the huge old trees and jumping over banks of dark ivy growing thick in the shadows.

They ran side by side through the grass, nipping playfully at each other. They played hide and seek, they played tag, they sniffed at flowers and ran after squirrels – never quite catching them. They stopped to drink at a low stone basin, ignoring the chatter and complaints of the birds bathing in the fountain.

And hiding, and chasing, and teasing, and playing, they finally arrived at the weed-grown yard that surrounded the old house. Benji's house.

Now it was Tiffany's home too.

SIX

Benji pushed his way through the honey-coloured dry grass. Tiffany followed in his wake, almost hidden by the tall weeds, until at last Benji stopped at a pile of wooden boxes and looked around. He barked once, then easily leapt from one box to another, up on to a rusty barrel, and on up, until he was standing on a low rail of the shaky old arbour.

Tiffany blinked in surprise, then unhappiness as Benji barked to indicate that she was to climb up, too.

She took a tentative leap up on to the lowest crate. Then up to a higher level. The third box rocked as she jumped on it, making her stop to catch her balance.

Benji woofed softly, urging her on. He ran up the lattice work and back down again to show her how easy and safe it was, but Tiffany still wore an anxious look on her face.

She finally jumped the distance from the barrel to the rail of the arbour, and looked around. Benji looked miles away above her. Slowly, slowly ... sure that every wiggle of the old trellis would send her crashing down

... Tiffany moved from one level to another. Finally there was just one more rail to go.

But it was much too high. She couldn't jump that far on to such a narrow ledge. Tiffany sat down, undecided what to do next. She looked behind her, but it was a long way down, and just as scary as the long way up.

Benji stood at the roof of the porch. He barked at her loudly and she stood, took a testing step forward, then backed up and sat down again. She whined sadly.

Barking encouragement, Benji paced back and forth along the edge of the roof.

Taking one last look at the ground so far below her, Tiffany rose and decided to face the challenge.

A carved bracket decorated the corner of the arbour where the lower part met the higher part at a right angle.

Stretching as far as she could, Tiffany hooked her tiny nails into the soft wood along the edge of the upper rail. Then, because she couldn't see her feet, she gingerly felt for footholds on the decorative trimming. First one foot, then the other, she moved very carefully ... very slowly.

Suddenly she slipped! Churning her short hind legs furiously, she hung over the side of the rail in space. The wood cracked under her front claws.

Benji stood frozen. He didn't dare risk jumping on the rail for fear the movement would shake Tiffany loose. He couldn't bark because his throat was tight with panic. Helplessly he watched Tiffany struggle to regain a foothold.

Miraculously, she did gain a foothold. One foot moved on to the bracket – then the other, as Tiffany panted for breath. Then she used all her strength to pull herself on to the top rail.

Benji went wild with pride and excitement. He barked and barked at the edge of the porch in admiration.

At last Tiffany stood up, and with slow, trembling steps and without looking down, her eyes fixed only on Benji, she crossed the narrow arbour and slowly but surely made it to the porch roof side. As she jumped up, Benji, bursting with love and admiration for her courage, nuzzled her and licked her nose and face.

From the porch roof he jumped on to the roof of the house, between the gables. Now Tiffany followed him without fear and they ran behind the house to Benji's upstairs window. Disappearing inside, he barked for her to follow. Tiffany stood on her hind legs and peered in through the broken pane. Benji woofed and backed out of the way, and in she jumped. They were home.

It was a strange, dark house, Tiffany decided, not like anything she had ever known before. It was filled with shadowy, bulky, shrouded objects and peculiar musty spells. She followed Benji across the landing, and down the winding stairs, avoiding, like Benji, the miniature painting that had fallen from the wall and was lying on the steps.

When they got downstairs, and into the centre of the vast foyer, Benji seemed beside himself with pride. He hardly knew what to show Tiffany first. He woofed, wagged his tail, and sneezed all at the same time, running round in circles in his excitement, as if to say, 'Well, here it is. What do you think?'

Tiffany didn't know quite what to think. She

began to sniff around cautiously, investigating the bases of the furniture, trying to recognise the various scents and aromas a dog's nose is so sensitive to. Meanwhile, Benji trotted over to the grocery bag the young people had left behind, the one he'd turned over before. Poking his shaggy head deep into the bag, he managed to nudge a pudding cup out. He woofed for Tiffany, and she came over to have a look. She sniffed at the cup, but couldn't find any smell because the cup was still sealed shut. She looked at Benji, puzzled.

Benji steadied the cup between his two front feet and pulled with his teeth at the little metal tab, as he'd seen Henry do yesterday. With a woof of triumph, he began to tug the lid open. It took some doing, but Tiffany was watching him, and he was showing off his skills for her. At last it was open, the lid was finally off. He laid the cup down and nudged it towards Tiffany. She took a tiny lick just to taste. Yum! Benji took his turn at the cup. Delicious!

The sudden sound of footsteps on the porch outside startled the dogs into freezing for an instant. Then, picking the pudding up in his teeth, Benji made a dash for the entrance to his 'nest', expecting that Tiffany would be close on his heels. But Tiffany, who had never learned to be afraid of human feet or of human voices, stood her ground, looking curiously at the front door.

Benji woofed at her in alarm.

'Do you think we should wait for him out here or go inside?' asked Henry's muffled voice outside the door.

Benji woofed again, more strongly this time.

'What was that?' Riley's voice held a note of fear.

Tiffany looked back at Benji, who ducked into his

nest to show her what he meant. But she was in no hurry.

'Whaddya mean, what was that?! A simple question! Should we wait out here or go on in? I say let's go on in.' Evidently, Henry had heard nothing.

Tiffany stood calmly at the centre of the room, waiting to see who was coming in.

'You go on in,' came Riley's voice. 'I'll stay out here for a while ... and then mosey on home.'

'Don't be silly. Come on!' urged Henry's voice.

The door opened at the touch of Henry's hand on the knob, and the sudden burst of light through the door caused Tiffany to scamper back towards Benji. The two young men came in, Henry carrying a thermos jug, Riley holding a box of stationery and a small bag with some paper cups sticking out of it. Whatever they were there for, they appeared to be well prepared. As Tiffany scurried into the nest, Benji drew his head back in. Both dogs watched from the shadows without a sound.

'I'm not being silly,' Riley protested. 'I heard something!'

'Maybe it was Mrs Powell's lovely head rolling down the stairs,' joked Henry in his best bogeyman voice.

'That does it!' Riley spun round and headed for the door again. Henry grabbed him by the shoulder.

'Knock it off,' he ordered. He shut the door and moved on into the foyer. 'Linda Sue and Mitch are going to walk in here and knock us both off this thing if you don't start acting like you've got some sense.'

'I've got plenty of sense,' spluttered Riley. 'It's guts I'm short of.' He looked round. 'I don't think I like this Mitch character anyway.'

60

Henry set the thermos jug down on the floor near the loveseat he'd sat in yesterday.

'For the kind of money we're getting, you don't have to like him.'

Riley balanced the stationery box on top of the jug and dropped the bag next to it. 'Well, I say if that's the best Linda Sue could do in the big city, she should've stayed at home.' Suddenly, he spotted the grocery bag lying on its side, its contents spilling out. 'Hey ... wait a minute! Come here, Henry. Look at this!'

'What about it?' Henry asked the other boy, coming to have a look.

'This bag wasn't dumped over like that yesterday.'

'Oh, come on, Riley. I told you to knock that stuff off. I'm going to look round upstairs.' Henry headed for the staircase.

'You can walk away calmly saying "knock it off" if you want to, but where's your pudding cup?'

'My what?' Henry turned back, puzzled.

'Didn't you leave a pudding cup sitting on the arm of that chair?' demanded Riley.

'I don't know. I probably took it with me!' Henry threw his hands up in the air, exasperated.

At that moment, the door opened again and Linda poked her pretty head through it. 'Yes, they're here,' she said to somebody behind her. She walked into the house, followed by a handsome man with blonde hair, older and somehow harder looking than Riley or Henry. There was something slick about him; Benji felt a warning prickle in the hairs at the back of his neck, but he kept silent. Both dogs watched the four people closely.

'Hi, Mitch,' said Riley.

'Hi,' echoed Henry.

'Hi, guys.' Mitch looked around him, his face lighting up with pleasure at what he saw. 'Hey, this place is super. Looks like an old haunted house right out of a movie.'

Linda grinned with pride. 'I knew you'd like it.' It was obvious that it was very important to her to please Mitch.

'And you're sure nobody ever comes here,' Mitch said.

'Just look around,' answered Linda. 'Nothing's been touched for years.'

'Except your pudding cup,' said Riley in a low voice to Henry.

Mitch whirled around. 'What was that?'

'I – uhhh – said – I think I'll eat a pudding cup.' Riley rummaged around in the grocery bag until he found the box.

Linda had moved into the sitting room. 'Look in here, Mitch.' She took Mitch by the hand and pulled him after her into the large parlour. Henry ambled in behind them.

'I thought this might be a good room to set up in,' explained Linda. 'It looks comfortable enough. And there are no windows,' she added. She looked about the room, as if to emphasise her point.

Mitch nodded his head in agreement. 'Yeah, this is great. It'll be good at night, too. It's shut off so we can have a light in here and no one can see it from the outside.'

'What're we in here at night for?' Henry wanted

to know. 'I thought we were going to be through before dark.'

Mitch shrugged lightly, as though it were a small detail, too unimportant to be discussed. 'Just covering all bases. You never know.'

Holding an open pudding cup in his hand, Riley walked into the parlour, a worried look on his face. He stirred the pudding, his hunger forgotten.

'Did I hear you mention dark?' he asked Henry in a whisper, so the others couldn't hear. 'And night?'

'Hey, look at this vase,' Linda called to Mitch from a corner of the room.

Henry shot Riley a look. 'Don't get in a nervous fidget, Riley. You're not goin' to have to be in here after dark.' Yet he glanced over at Mitch, who was inspecting the furniture with Linda. 'Or, at least, that's the plan,' he added, a small tinge of doubt creeping into his words.

'That must be a hundred years old!' cried Mitch. 'The stuff in this place must be worth a fortune.' He opened the door that led from the parlour to an indoor garden beyond. 'What's out here?'

'I think it's just a sun porch,' answered Linda, following him out.

As Mitch and Linda left the parlour, Riley grabbed at Henry's sleeve and tugged him nervously back into the foyer, signalling him to be quiet.

'Come 'ere. Plan or no plan I ain't staying in this place after dark,' he whispered urgently. 'Listen, how many puddings are in a carton?'

'What?' Henry's face wore a 'what-kind-of-a-question-is-that?' look.

But Riley pressed on, waving his pudding cup

63

under Henry's nose for emphasis. 'How many pudding cups come in one of those little cardboard cartons?'

'How should I know!'

'You bought it! Think about it,' Riley urged. 'It's important.'

'Henry cast his eyes up to heaven. 'Four ... I guess,' he said.

Riley nodded grimly. 'That's what I thought. There's one missing.'

Henry breathed a deep sigh. He was really getting tired of all this. 'What do you mean there's one missing?' he asked slowly.

Riley held up the fingers of one hand to count. 'You ate one yesterday and I'm eating this one so there should be two in the carton, right?'

Henry was bored with the whole conversation. 'How many, Riley?' he asked.

Riley showed a single finger. 'One,' he said. He was like Sherlock Holmes trying to solve a tricky problem.

'They could have shorted us at the shop,' Henry offered. He idly wondered if the grandfather clock would still run.

Riley shook his head. 'You'd've noticed it. I tell you something's wrong with this place.'

But Henry wasn't buying that story. 'Don't be silly, Riley. There's a logical answer for it. The carton was short. It fell out of the bag. Or something!'

Both boys turned as they heard the door of the sun porch open and shut.

'Now don't bug anyone about it,' Henry warned Riley in a low voice. He pushed him gently into a nearby chair. 'Just sit down and look relaxed and ... keep quiet!' He strolled over to a sculptured marble figure and pretended to be examining the dust on it as Mitch and Linda came back into the foyer.

'Do you want to see the rest of the house?' Linda asked Mitch, looping her arm through his.

'No need to. This is all we'll use and it's perfect.'

'So this is definitely the place, huh?' Henry asked Mitch matter-of-factly.

Mitch nodded. 'This is it. You know the time and schedule, right?'

'Right,' nodded Henry.

'O.K. I'm off to the city. I'll see you guys tomorrow,' said Mitch. He and Linda moved towards the front door. 'You go on back to your parents' house, and I'll see you in a few weeks,' Mitch told her.

'I'll miss you,' Linda whispered softly.

Mitch shrugged. 'I'll miss you, too, but it's going to be worth it.' The front door shut behind them.

Henry stood awhile, listening to the silence of the old house, then he turned to his friend. 'Come on. Let's get out of here.'

'I can't think of anything I'd rather do,' agreed Riley. He took a final bite from the pudding cup, and looked inside to make certain that some dessert was left. Gesturing to Henry with the cup, he said, 'Note.' He set the half-filled cup carefully down on the arm of the chair. 'I'm leaving it right here,' he told Henry. 'On purpose.'

'And I'm sure it'll be right there tomorrow, on purpose, too,' Henry said. He placed his hand on the doorknob. 'Unless, of course, Mrs Powell's lovely head gets hungry.'

Riley scrambled for the door. 'I really wish you wouldn't talk like that.' The door groaned shut behind them in a cloud of dust.

Benji and Tiffany were alone together at last. But for them, it had been a long day, and the most exciting day in their young lives. So far. Curled up together in Benji's nest, both dogs were soon fast asleep.

SEVEN

Cindy's sobs grew louder and louder, even though she was trying hard to control them. Tears burned their way down her cheeks and fell in tiny drops from her trembling chin, making dark smudges on the collar of her blue shirt. She was thoroughly miserable and really didn't care who knew it. It just wasn't fair, that was all! Paul was having trouble keeping his own tears back.

'But, Daddy, *why*?' he begged for the third time.

Dr Chapman tried to keep his patience. He loved these two kids more than anything in the world and he wanted only what was best for them; why couldn't he make them understand that!

'That's just the way it has to be, son,' he explained warmly but firmly. 'We don't know what he gets into ... what germs he's carrying around ... or really anything about him. He could be picking up diseases all over town and bringing 'em here.' Outside on the porch, Benji and Tiffany sat quietly waiting for Cindy and Paul to come out and play.

Caught! The three had been caught in the act of

feeding strays. And what was worse, not one stray but two! Even Mary was close to tears, her worst fears having come true.

'But, Daddy, he's not!' sobbed Cindy. 'We know!'

'Honey, you never know,' replied her father. 'You can't see disease. Believe me, I've been there and it's not worth the risk to the family. I'll get you any kind of dog you want and we'll build a fence around the back . . .'

'We don't want any kind of dog,' Cindy cried. 'We want *Benji*! Why can't we build a fence for Benji?'

'Mary and I talked about that . . . and . . . well . . .' Dr Chapman looked at his housekeeper for support. Mary sighed.

'I said I thought it would be cruel.'

'Why?' bawled Cindy.

Mary reached out and pulled Cindy into her arms. 'Honey, Benji's a very special kind of dog and he's been on his own for a long time. I think he would be very, very unhappy if you penned him up.'

Mary could see that Cindy didn't understand and she wasn't sure that she did herself, but she kept trying. 'That's the hardest part of love sometimes. Doing what you know is best for the one you love even though it hurts you a whole lot.'

It didn't help. Love couldn't hurt this much, Cindy thought fleetingly, but Mary continued.

'That's what your father is trying to do for you and that's what you should do for Benji . . . if you love him.'

Through a haze of tears, Cindy looked from Mary to her father. How could they know? How could they understand . . . and how could they do this to her?

Cindy cried out, 'It's just not fair!' She ran to the screen door, pushed it open and stumbled down the steps into the back yard. Benji stood and followed her out, Tiffany sat quietly on the porch, waiting, somehow understanding.

Dr Chapman turned to his son. 'Paul ... try to understand,' he pleaded.

Paul shook his head, fighting back the tears. 'I'm trying, Dad. I just can't.'

His father suddenly felt that he had run out of words. He sat silent for a long minute, then said gently to Paul, 'Maybe you'd better go and look after your sister.'

Paul tried hard to think of something to say – one word that could make his father see. But his mind was blurred and his eyes were burning. He slowly pushed open the screen door and went to look for Cindy. Dr Chapman came to the door to watch. It was breaking his heart to see his two kids so unhappy. And over two ordinary dogs! What do you do with kids, anyway?

'Mary, how do you know when you're right or wrong?' he sighed. 'Am I really doing what's best? ... or am I just being a rotten heel?' He gazed through the screen, watching Paul walking sadly away.

Mary had no answers and she knew it. What was there to say? After a long moment of silence, she mumbled. 'No, sir ... and yes, sir.'

Cindy lay crying quietly, curled up under a bush so that the world would never find her. But Benji knew the bush. He poked his whiskered face into the shrubbery and licked her tear-stained cheeks. Looking up at him with watery eyes, she gave a little cry and reached out, hugging him tightly to her chest. Paul found them both there, and knelt down beside them. Benji rewarded him with a bark and a lick, too, and Paul ruffled the dog's shaggy head in return.

Slowly the three came out from under the bush and into the sunlight. They began to walk back to the house, Benji leading the way and Cindy following very slowly, tears still trickling one by one down her cheeks. Running from one to the other, Benji leaped into the air and turned somersaults. Anything to make Cindy laugh. He jumped at Paul and nearly knocked him down; that brought him the payment of a tiny smile – just the beginnings of one – from Cindy.

Benji spotted a red ball and brought it to Paul, barking with excitement. Paul threw it. Benji bounded over the grass to bring it back and suddenly, they were all laughing. As they romped over the lawn, tears seemed to be forgotten.

But Benji couldn't stay long. He was behind schedule. Today was the day that Tiffany was to meet all his friends. He called her to his side with a woof, and they turned to go. As they barked goodbye, Cindy's eyes filled up again and Paul felt a lump in his throat. Then the two furry bodies wriggled through the broken place in the fence and were gone.

'Come on,' Paul told his sister. 'Let's get to school. A few minutes with Miss Gildy can take our minds off anything.'

Brother and sister walked slowly towards the house.

The Finster cat was watching the two dogs suspiciously as they romped across her yard, nipping at each other playfully. Her muscles tensed for the leap up in the air and the dash for the tree she would make in a second. But the leap and the dash never came. Benji was too busy to chase her this morning; he was busy playing with Tiffany. As both dogs began to scamper out of the yard, the cat gave one loud, lonely miaow of neglect.

Mrs Finster was watering her roses, but she turned immediately to join in the daily game. 'You stay away from my cat, you malicious –' The old lady broke off short. The cat was sitting alone on the tree stump, her tail drooping sadly.

'Well, where is he, Sweetie-Peetie?' she asked.

The cat just looked at her with big yellow eyes and twitched her whiskers. Mrs Finster looked around the yard, spotting Benji romping off with Tiffany.

'Why, you poor thing!' she exclaimed to her pet. 'Is he ignoring you?' She brandished her fist at Benji, yelling, 'You come back here and chase my cat this minute, you irresponsible, inconsiderate rogue!' She gathered the Persian into her arms for comfort. 'Do you want to give her a complex?!' But Benji and Tiffany were out of hearing.

Tiffany had to trot faster to keep up with Officer Tuttle's long legs; Benji was used to Tuttle's stride. The fountain near the civic centre sparkled in the sunshine. Children's voices rose into the air as they played their baby games around the merry tree.

'Well, Butch, you sure move fast. And you sure got yourself a pretty little thing,' the policeman said, with an approving look at Tiffany. The trio headed for Tuttle's favourite bench.

'O.K., sit up,' the officer ordered, and Benji obeyed, catching the popcorn reward in his mouth on the fly.

'That's good,' said Tuttle. 'Now *all* the way up.'

Benji stood up on his hind legs and took a few steps forward. It was Tuttle's favourite trick.

'That's a good boy.' He leaned forward to give Benji some popcorn and whispered, 'She's trying to hide it, but I can tell she's impressed.'

'Now you understand I mean no offence to your young lady friend here.' said old Bill, as he patted the two heads in his lap, 'but I feel my many years of experience obligates me to tell you to think long and hard about this thing, because a woman surely ties a man down.' He peered over his glasses at Tiffany, then at Benji. ''Course, as I recall, they generally make it worth while,' he grinned to Benji with a wink.

'Another thing.' Bill came back out of the cafe with two juicy bones, and handed one to each. 'It's a lot of bunk, that saying "two can live as cheaply as one".'

Benji's last stop was at the litter basket, his own private litter basket in his own private little park. Today, it was especially important to him; this was the very spot where he and Tiffany had met only yesterday. And so he was especially gallant; having tipped it over, he allowed Tiffany to go first. And there must have been something especially good to eat in there, too, for she tumbled in head-first in her excitement. Well, she'll have to learn, thought Benji . . . but there would be plenty of time for that. Plenty of time.

And now they were home again, standing side by side

72

at the foot of the tall arbour. Tiffany thought, 'Oh no. Not again.' But her faith in Benji was complete, and she no longer felt fear. Suddenly Benji whirled about. He had decided to show her his greatest treasure. He woofed at Tiffany to follow him, and with a jaunty trot, he led her around the staircase to a small shack that stood behind the house. In the shack was an old, leather suitcase. Tugging at the strap with his teeth, Benji lifted the lid. Bones – big bones, little bones, meaty bones, chewy bones. It was a king's ransom! Let other, common dogs bury their bones in the ground. Not Benji! He deposited his bone in the case, carefully laid Tiffany's beside it, and nudged the lid shut. Then, side by side, they left the shack and carefully climbed the arbour to the broken window on the second floor of the house.

'I told you it wouldn't be there, Henry!' Riley's voice rose until it cracked. 'I told you that pudding cup would be gone. And I'm fixing to be gone with it!'

At the first sound of Riley's voice, Benji braked to a stop upstairs, Tiffany bumping into him from the rear. He crouched down low, and proceeded slowly, cautiously, out of the bedroom and down the steps to the halfway landing. Tiffany kept well behind. Peering through the cobwebs on the banister railings, Benji watched the two young men below him in the foyer. They appeared to be arguing.

'You've said that three times,' shouted Henry, out of patience. 'Now will you please shut up and write! We're running late.'

'Well,' demanded Riley, 'Where did it go?'

'Maybe we've got trained pudding cups! How

should I know? Probably some kid found that door open.'

Benji poked his nose through the banisters. The man called Riley was sitting at a large old table in the foyer, awkwardly trying to write with his left hand on a piece of lavender paper from the open stationery box. On the floor, next to the thermos jug, were a couple of screwed up sweet papers and a used paper cup.

'You find me a kid that'll even walk *into* this place and that *ain't* the kid that's going to do absolutely nothing but walk off with one half-eaten pudding cup!' Riley waved his arm for emphasis as he talked, raising dust and cobwebs.

'Write!' Henry pointed to the table.

Riley turned back to his paper. 'This'd be hard enough to do if I were safe at home, but it's practically impossible under these circumstances.'

Henry looked over Riley's shoulder. 'It's working, though,' he commented.

'What do you mean?'

'I mean it's working,' stated Henry with just a touch of sarcasm. 'Doing it left-handed so they can't trace the handwriting!' He snatched up the paper off the table. 'They can't even *read* it, so how could they trace it?!' He screwed up the paper in disgust, and threw it on the floor. 'Move!' he ordered Riley. 'Let me do it.'

Riley stood up and stalked off in the direction of the stairs. Seeing him coming, Benji ducked down out of sight.

'I'm sorry, Henry,' Riley blurted out. 'I don't like this *place*. I don't even think I like this *deal* ... and I'm just nervous, that's all.' He turned to face his friend, and Benji's head popped up again, peering through the banisters.

'We don't have time to be nervous,' retorted Henry, writing. The pick-up should have already been made and Mitch'll be back before long. We've got to get you in position.' He put a finishing touch to the note. 'Now, look at that,' he said proudly, waving the paper to dry. 'No problem at all if you concentrate on what you're doing instead of worrying about pudding cups.' Henry folded the note, handed it to Riley, and stood up. Benji ducked back down again.

'Here,' said Henry. 'You know where to go.'

Riley moved slowly towards the door. 'Yeah, I'll trade this place for a phone booth any day. What time?'

Henry checked his watch. 'If you don't hear from me in forty-five minutes, make the delivery.'

'O.K.' Riley closed the front door behind him.

Henry turned back from the door, shaking his head at Riley's silliness. He looked round the foyer, wondering what to do with himself for the next three-quarters of an hour. Heading for the sitting room he went to the bookshelves and searched for something to read.

Benji poked his head around the corner of the landing and checked out the foyer. All quiet. He made his way down the stairs slowly, Tiffany following. They stopped at each step, all their canine senses alert, waiting for the next thing to happen. But nothing did.

Henry had found an old book that interested him, and he carried it over to a sofa, plopping down on it with his feet up on the armrest. Beji and Tiffany had reached the bottom of the stairs now, and crept quietly out into the foyer. At the door of the parlour, he stood frozen, watching. The man seemed to be completely wrapped up in his book, and all was still quiet.

Feeling a bit more secure, Benji decided to check out a few more of the things on the floor. Tiffany was already sniffing at a sweet paper, as Benji took a smell at the thermos. Then he moved over to Riley's note, which Henry had crumpled and thrown away.

The note was too screwed up to read the whole thing. But certain words stood out clearly. '£50,000 by 7 p.m.,' read one line. And another said, '. . . never see your kids again.' If only Benji could read, he might have known what was about to come.

Footsteps sounded on the porch. Benji, startled, made a quick dash for his nest, Tiffany right at his heels. He could hear a scuffling sound, as though there were many feet on the porch, and muffled voices. He recognised Mitch's voice from yesterday, and his neck-fur prickled again. Benji surely didn't like this man.

'Can't you move any faster than that?' Mitch's voice rose in anger. 'Hurry up!'

Benji could see the light shine in strongly as the front door was opened, and he heard Linda's voice, distressed and pleading, almost filled with tears.

'Mitch, this is wrong! This is not the way we planned it! Why did you change your mind?'

'Shut up and close the door,' Mitch growled, and Benji growled, too. But too softly to be heard. The door slammed shut.

'Now get in here and stop your squirming, or somebody's going to get hurt!' Mitch sounded really angry.

Suddenly, Benji sat up straight, every nerve in his body tingling. Mitch had pushed two kids into the middle of the foyer. They stood there, trembling, frightened half to death, their young eyes wide with terror, white gags stretched cruelly over their mouths.

Benji's heart gave a leap.

They were Paul and Cindy Chapman!

EIGHT

'Hey, what is this?!' Henry, surprised and angry, lurched through the sitting room doorway. 'What're they doing here?'

'Shut up!' snarled Mitch. 'Linda, take 'em in the other room!'

'I won't shut up!' Henry raised his voice. 'They're supposed to be out in the country, looking at a horse!'

Paul and Cindy stood huddled together, hardly daring to look round. They had no idea of what was going to happen to them, but everything they could think of was worse than everything else.

'Now what are they doing here?' Henry demanded. 'Linda ...'

Benji's mind was in a turmoil. He couldn't decide what to do; whether to go out and ... what? Why were they here? He knew it wasn't good. He took a few steps out of his nest; then turned back and hid himself again so that he could observe without being seen himself. Tiffany remained crouched down, her eyes frequently turning from the action to Benji, questioning.

Linda was near tears. 'I don't know, Henry. I promise I don't know. It's Mitch . . .'

'Well, Mitch better explain fast or Mitch'll have this whole thing in his lap!'

Henry was now standing nose to nose with Mitch. 'I bargained for a simple con job,' he argued. *'Not kidnapping!'*

'Well, you've got *kidnapping*! All of you!' Mitch stuck his nose against Henry's. 'You and your buddy write the note!' He turned angrily to Linda. 'You made the pick-up . . . And I've never even been seen in this town! Do you get the picture?' He turned again to glare at Paul and Cindy. 'Now get these kids in there like I said!' He shoved the kids hard in the direction of the sitting room; Paul bumped into Cindy and she fell.

With a snarl, Benji leaped to his feet and ran from his nest into the passageway. There, common sense got the better of him and he stopped, and slowly moved half way back again. Then, still undecided about what he could do, he turned one more time and paused at the corner of the foyer, peering round it cautiously.

'You don't have to shove 'em around,' stated Linda, helping Cindy to her feet. She spoke gently to the kids. 'Come on. Let's go in there.'

'And don't take your eyes off 'em,' Mitch ordered. He followed them to the sitting room door. 'In fact, put 'em in those two chairs over there so we can see 'em from either room.'

Henry began to sidle slowly towards the front door, his eyes on his watch.

'Can I take these gags off?' asked Linda, settling Cindy and Paul into deep armchairs.

'One sound and they go back on.' Mitch turned from the doorway in time to see Henry with his hand almost on the knob. 'Where do you think you're going?'

Henry turned from the front door. 'Look. I don't like this set up one bit ... but what's done is done, and if we want that ransom I've got to go and call the "deliver" signal to Riley.'

Mitch shook his head in bitter amusement. 'Henry ... Henry ... Henry ... Surely you haven't forgotten that it's *my* plan. *No* signal means "deliver".'

Henry thought furiously. 'Yeah, but we changed it. I mean, you might've had a flat tyre or something before the pick up.'

Mitch shook his head again. 'Not true, Henry. Come on back.'

Henry took a chance and made a break for the door. 'No way,' he yelled.

'Hold it! I'll shoot!'

Henry froze in astonishment. Mitch was actually holding a gun on him – a real gun. This was no amateur con game, no practical joke. It was a real gun and this was a real crime and he, Henry, was in it up to his neck. He looked from the cold steel of the gun to the cold steel in Mitch's eyes and shuddered. He wasn't sure which was more dangerous, more to be feared. But he'd bet on the eyes.

Benji's eyes were glued to the gun, too. A grip of fear caught him around his heart, squeezing the breath out of him. A gun. Somehow he knew about guns. Somehow and somewhere ... long ago ...

... He was a pup then. It was starting to come back to him. He'd been a pup and he hadn't always been independent. Once there had been a Someone, Someone he'd walked with, run to at a whistle ... somebody who had fed him every day, and made room for him on the bed at night. Benji remembered now. Someone had been a policeman, young, tall, and strong. Like Officer Tuttle.

They had been walking together. It was a chilly night and Benji was trotting by his side. They approached a corner, turned it ... Benji tried to shut the memory out now, but it was too strong for him. Yes, a man was breaking into a store. The policeman had called out to him. But just then a pistol, just like the one Mitch was holding on Henry ...

Benji couldn't bear to think of the rest. The noise. And – his policeman was lying there. Looking at the gun, Benji remembered it all. And he trembled in fear and confusion, and backed into his nest again, crawling in next to Tiffany.

'In a few minutes, that note'll be delivered and you'll all be in this thing together.' Mitch's voice held a note of smug satisfaction. 'So let's just relax until Riley gets back. Then I won't have to worry about you too much.' He waved the gun in the direction of the sitting room and Henry followed it slowly.

'In there,' commanded Mitch. 'Sit down somewhere.'

Henry's fear began to turn to anger as he saw how scared the Chapman children were. Cindy was weeping silently, and Paul's eyes were wet, although he was still struggling to hold back the tears.

Back at the nest, Benji was pacing back and forth. Tiffany watched him quietly. She could offer nothing in the way of help or advice. But Benji felt the urgent need to act. No more time for indecision. He started down the passageway that led to the foyer and peered round the corner. He could see nobody; the foyer was empty.

'Mitch,' he heard Linda say softly.

'What?'

Benji moved step by cautious step into the foyer, keeping his body close to the wall, his eyes glued to the sitting room door.

'Why?' Her voice trembled with sadness. 'Why couldn't we have done it the way we planned?'

Benji slid under a chair for cover. Nothing moved, and he continued down the foyer, still hugging the wall. At last he turned the corner and eased up behind the silent grandfather clock standing guard next to the sitting room.

'It wouldn't have worked,' Mitch explained. 'There wasn't enough time. He couldn't get a hundred thousand in this town by seven o'clock if his *own* life depended on it.'

'You said he could before,' Linda pointed out. 'You wouldn't have done it otherwise. None of you would. So I did you a favour.'

'Don't do me any more, O.K.?' said Henry with bitterness.

As Benji peered out from behind the clock, seeing Cindy and Paul in armchairs, and Henry, Mitch, and Linda on the sofa, Mitch sprang to his feet and headed for the door. In an instant, Benji was behind the clock again, his heart beating like a hammer.

'Well, I think I'll see what kind of groceries you've got in the bags out there.' Mitch turned in the doorway. 'And don't get any clever ideas, Henry!'

As he bent to rummage in the paper bags, Benji made a fast dash up the stairs, hoping Mitch would not turn and see him.

He made it to the first landing safely, but, rushing on his way up to the second floor, his paw hit the miniature painting that had been lying on the steps. It went spinning and clattered down the stairs.

Mitch looked up at the sound; Benji froze, his heart in his mouth. Mitch strained to hear the echoes. Quietly getting up, he listened a moment longer, then moved towards the door. Pulling back the curtain, he looked out. Nothing. He came back to the stairs, where Benji lay crouched, out of sight. Mitch looked up. Nothing. Nothing unusual. A falling shingle perhaps? That wouldn't be unusual in an old house. Deciding that his imagination had been playing him tricks, Mitch returned to the groceries.

Benji lay very still on the stairs, listening to Mitch's footsteps recede. Then, inch by inch, he made it to the upstairs bedroom. Quietly now, out of the window and on to the porch. Then the roof, the trellis, the lattice work, and the boxes. He was on the ground. He'd made it. Free.

Now to the Chapman house!

NINE

Nobody was coming to the door. Benji had scratched and barked until his paws and his throat were tired, but nobody came. Where was Mary? Where, even, was Dr Chapman? Benji would take his chances with the doctor, if only he could get somebody's attention. But nobody was paying any attention to the tired, dusty dog scratching at the Chapman screen door.

Benji pawed at the door one last time; then, using his front foot as a lever the way he'd taught himself, he pushed the screen door open and went into the empty kitchen. No one. Crossing the large room, he stopped at the swinging door that led to the hallway and the house beyond. Here he hesitated a moment. Outside that swinging door was forbidden territory; Benji had never been past the Chapman kitchen in his life. But he had no choice.

He lightly scratched at the door. Nothing. Then he nuzzled it, pushing hard with his head and shoulders. It wasn't hard to do; the door swung open just enough for Benji to squeeze through it and out into the hall.

The long hallway was beautifully furnished and

decorated with handsome wallpaper and beautiful paintings. But Benji saw nothing of that; in the distance, at the end of the hallway, he could hear voices. Human voices. Cautiously he made his way down the corridor towards the sound.

'Do they always walk home?' a strange man's voice was asking.

'Unless the weather's bad.' That was Mary's voice, but different. Muffled, sad, as though she'd been crying hard.

'Do you know if they usually take the same route every day?'

'Depends on whether they have any money or not. If their pockets are empty, they'll take the quickest possible way, to get home for a snack. That would be straight down Ridgewood or Mill Valley and across to Tennessee. If they've got money, it's straight to Bessel's Store.'

Benji had reached the end of the corridor and stood looking in at the large Chapman living room. It was filled with people. In the far corner of the room Dr Chapman and Mary were being questioned by Lieutenant Samuels, a plain clothes officer. Another plain clothes man was talking to Mr and Mrs Harvey, an older couple, while Bob Fielding, a man about Dr Chapman's age, was sitting on the couch drinking coffee. There were also two uniformed policemen in the room. One of them, Floyd Dullen, was talking on the telephone, while the other, Tom Hatcher, stood silently by awaiting instructions. Here was help enough!

'Did they have money this morning?' asked Lieutenant Samuels.

'Yes, they did,' replied Dr Chapman. He turned to Mary. 'I game 'em some to try to soften that business with the dog,' he explained.

'Excuse me a minute,' said Mary, and stood up to help herself to a glass of water from a nearby serving tray. Benji spotted her and his heart gave a leap of joy. Mary would fix everything! He started to go to her, across the living room floor, but as he passed the coffee table, a familiar smell caught his attention, and he turned to sniff a piece of lavender paper on the table.

'Benji!' cried Mary, as she caught sight of the dog.

Benji looked up at Mary and began to bark, loudly and urgently.

'What are you doing in here?!' She rushed across the room to him, bent down and picked him up in her arms. 'You're a bad dog!' Turning to Dr Chapman, she apologised. 'I'm sorry, doctor! I can't imagine ... he's never been past the kitchen before.' Almost running, she carried Benji out of the living room, down the hallway to the kitchen and through the screen door. Dumping him firmly on the back porch, she shooed him away. 'Shame on you! Now run along!'

But Benji wouldn't discourage so easily. He barked at her, quickly, loudly, a barrage of urgent barks, then he started down the steps.

'No!' said Mary. 'I don't have time to play with you. Now go on.' She turned to go back into the house and Benji's frantic barks became a long whine. Mary's face softened. She opened the screen door, and came out to pet him a little.

'Look,' she said gently, 'I know you can't understand but we've got a lot to worry about in here and we

86

don't have time to play. And we don't need any extra problems, see?'

If only she would listen! If only she would follow him! He woofed at her loudly, his 'follow-me' woof, that worked so well on Tiffany. Then he ran off across the back yard.

'That's a good boy,' said Mary, and she went back inside the house. The screen door slammed shut.

Benji turned. Mary was gone. He ran swiftly back to the house, barking at the top of his lungs. Nobody came. Running back up to the porch steps, he opened the screen door, crossed the kitchen and nuzzled the swinging door open a second time. Getting Mary's attention hadn't worked. But he had to do something.

The hallway was empty. Good. Benji crept down the corridor as quietly as he could, every sense on the alert. A door suddenly opened ahead of him and he dived for the cover of a nearby table. Mary came out of the door, heading for the living room. Benji's head popped up. He longed to go to her, to try again to make her understand, but all his instincts told him that it wouldn't work this time, either. No, he had to think of a better plan. He sneezed in frustration, then turned himself in a circle, as dogs do when they are trying to think. He lay down, dropping his head on his paws, and stared off into space. Wasn't there anything he could do? After a minute he decided to move back down the corridor to a better vantage point.

He moved more quickly down the corridor, his gaze fixed on the living room at the end of it. Still, he kept to the wall, seeking the cover of the furniture. At the end of the hallway was a large, leafy plant that made a good hiding place, yet he could see everything that was happening in the living room. He kept very still. Only his eyes were visible through the leaves of the plant, black eyes glittering brightly with excitement, and glued to what was taking place in the next room.

'Why don't you relax for a minute, doctor?' Lieutenant Samuels was saying. 'But we'll need to go over all this again when the agent gets here.' The plain clothes detective stood up and walked over to the officer, who was still listening intently to an open line on the phone.

'Floyd, have you heard anything on the FBI guy?'

'Just that there's one on the way,' replied the policeman.

'It'll probably take him forever at this time of day. What about the patrols?'

The officer shook his head. 'Nothing.'

'And the phone?' Samuels continued. 'What does it take to get those phone people moving? We've got to free this line!'

'They're working on it,' Floyd said. 'Shouldn't be long.'

'Well, maybe you'd better go out and use the radio until they get in.'

'O.K. Floyd nodded. 'Wait a minute ...' Something was coming through at the other end of the phone. 'Yes, Fred. Go ahead.' He began to write.

Mary was pouring Dr Chapman a cup of coffee, and murmuring low apologies about Benji's interruption. The doctor shook his head tiredly. 'Don't worry about it; that dog is the least of my concerns right now.' He moved over to join Bob Fielding on the couch, and Mary turned her attention to clearing up the tray, nervously stacking napkins and rearranging coffee cups that were already neatly placed.

'Any word?' Chapman asked Bob.

'Yes. I think I've got it worked out at the bank, unless they want the money in special denominations,' Fielding replied. 'Then we may have a problem.'

'Nobody?' Floyd asked into the phone. 'Yep, O.K.' He turned to the lieutenant. 'Nothing on the people. So far, nobody's seen anything.'

The front doorbell rang loudly.

'I'll get it,' called Mary, dropping a pile of napkins on the tray. Benji scooted down as far as he could to keep hidden.

'No, I'll get it, Mary,' Lieutenant Samuels said. He went to the door and opened it. A short, greying, dishevelled man was standing there. His narrow striped tie was loose at the neck and, although the day was very warm, he wore a suit.

'Yes?' asked Samuels.

'Payton Murrah. FBI.' His voice was rough but friendly, Benji decided.

Samuels grasped his right hand in a firm handshake. 'You got here quicker than I expected. Ted Samuels. Silver Creek Police. Come on in.'

As they walked towards the living room, Samuels commented, 'You must have been half way here when they called you.'

Murrah smiled. 'I almost was. I live out this way.'

'Dr Chapman, this is Payton Murrah of the FBI.'

'Doctor,' Payton Murrah said, shaking hands.

'How do you do?'

'His attorney, Bob Fielding.' Lieutenant Samuels continued the introductions.

'Mr Fielding.' Another firm handshake.

'His housekeeper, Mary Grubber. She's also been a sort of governess to the kids since the doctor lost his wife.'

'Mary.'

'That's Dr Chapman's sister and brother-in-law, Mr and Mrs Harvey. This is Officer Floyd Dullen, and Officer Tom Hatcher,' Samuels said. 'I guess we should start at the beginning and work our way up to what we've accomplished so far,' Samuels said. 'Floyd, where's the note?'

'Over here.' Floyd picked up the ransom note off the coffee table. It was the piece of paper that Benji had sniffed at, knowing there was something familiar about it. Out in the hallway, Benji's head perked up sharply as his eyes riveted on the note. He watched closely as Floyd handed it to Lieutenant Samuels, who passed it on to the FBI man. Murrah looked at it carefully, front and back.

'This is the ransom note,' Lieutenant Samuels said as Murrah read it. 'There weren't any prints. And we haven't heard on the handwriting yet.'

'Hmmm,' the FBI man pondered. 'How was it delivered?' He handed the note to Samuels and, out in the hall, Benji kept his eyes glued to the piece of paper.

'Doctor, would you go over it one more time?' Samuels requested.

'Yes, of course. I received a call at my office that was supposedly from Cindy's school, telling me that Cindy had been in an accident. They asked me if I could come to the nurse's office at once. When I got to my car, the note was stuck to the windscreen.' Dr Chapman's thoughts seemed far away.

'I see,' said the FBI man, understanding the pain the doctor was going through.

Benji's eyes were still glued to the note as Samuels handed it to Floyd, who dropped it on to a nearby table. Benji thought it was now or never. He bolted from his hiding place and raced towards the table. Seizing the note between his teeth he spun round and ran back towards the hall.

'The note!' yelled Floyd. 'The note!'

He made a grab for Benji, but missed as the dog darted back down the hallway.

'It's that dog!' Samuels shouted.

'He's got the note!'

'Benji!' That was Mary.

'Get him!' yelled Samuels.

Halfway down the hall, Benji paused just long enough to encourage them to follow, then he made a dash for the kitchen, Floyd right on his heels. Behind him, Benji could hear a roomful of people shouting and running; everybody was after him! He dashed down the hall, clutching the note firmly in his teeth. The hallway seemed endless, but at last he reached the kitchen, bursting through the door, and scampering across the shiny linoleum. Benji leaped up, slamming into the screen door, and pushing it open. Like a flash, he was through it, only inches ahead of Floyd's grasping hands. Floyd stumbled on the doorstep and nearly fell, but he managed to get through the door, his hands reaching for Benji.

Not waiting to run down the steps, Benji took them all in one flying leap, widening his lead by only a little, and headed round the corner for the hole in the front yard fence. He took one quick look round to check his pursuers. Floyd was gaining on him, his long legs eating up the ground, but some of the others were dropping back, out of condition and winded.

The hole in the fence was just round the next corner now. Benji made a painful burst of effort and picked up a little speed. He rounded the corner for the last lap and ran ... smack into Lieutenant Samuel's legs and outstretched hands. Samuels hadn't chased Benji; he'd come out of the front door and cut him off.

'Gotcha!' cried the detective.

Benji's plan had failed.

TEN

Lieutenant Samuels' strong hands held Benji tightly by the shoulders. Out of breath, Floyd galloped up and grabbed Benji by his back legs. Reaching into Benji's mouth, the police detective removed the ransom note from the dog's teeth.

'You know you'd have caused a great deal of trouble if you'd run off with this,' Samuels scolded Benji.

'He would've gone, too, if you hadn't been here,' panted Floyd.

Mary, holding her side where a stitch had grabbed her, came puffing up, her face red with the strain of running.

'What's the deal with this dog, Mary?' asked Samuels. 'Does he belong around here?'

'No, not really.'

'You want us to take care of him?'

Mary looked hard at Benji. He could see she was really angry with him. 'I've got half a mind to say yes.' Benji's eyes pleaded mutely, and Mary turned her head away. 'But I guess I won't. Just let him go.'

The policemen released Benji and headed back towards the house. Mary, still out of breath, her side hurting, turned back to the dog, who sat silent on the grass, unable to get his urgent message across.

'What's got into you? You act like you've gone crazy!' A frown drew two sharp lines between her usually laughing eyes. 'I don't want to be unkind to you, Benji, but I'm going to have to be if you cause any more trouble.' She started back to the house, then turned and pointed sharply at the street. 'Now go home! Or wherever you go.'

She disappeared round the hedge, leaving Benji alone. He just sat there, head down, ears drooping in complete misery. Why wouldn't they understand? Where could he go now and find help? He got slowly to his feet and dragged himself through the hole in the fence, moping off down the street.

Benji still believed that he needed human help. But who? Mary would hand him to the police for sure the next time he barged in there. It would be getting dark pretty soon. The only one left was Bill, old Bill. He was ancient and feeble, but he was human, and that was better than nothing. Dolefully, Benji headed for Bill's Cafe.

The old wooden chair in front of the cafe was empty. And a sign hung from the plate-glass window, reading CLOSED. Benji climbed up into the chair, completely exhausted. He was ready to cry. The frustration was too much. He laid his head on his paws and sighed deeply. He had tried his very best, but nothing had worked. Nobody could understand what he wanted to tell them. He jumped down from the chair and headed for the park.

Benji had come to his usual bench in the park near

the Civic Centre. His head drooped sadly over the side of the bench. Officer Tuttle was nowhere to be seen. Dejected and completely defeated, Benji saw nothing, heard nothing of the laughter and play in the park. Around him, everything was growing dark and forbidding.

Outside the Municipal Building that housed the police force of Silver Creek, Officer Tuttle was overtaken by Attorney Fred Johnson. They headed down the pavement together, walking slowly.

'Hey, Tuttle, you heard about the Chapman kids?' asked Johnson.

The handsome face of the young black man grew sad. 'Yep, that's a really bad scene.'

'You working on it?'

'No, the lieutenant's handling it himself, and he's got Floyd and Tom with him.'

'Why Chapman?' Johnson wanted to know. 'How much could they expect to get from him?'

The sound of their voices reached Benji's ears. Both his ears cocked at once. Tuttle! It was Officer Tuttle, his friend!

In a flash, Benji dived off the bench and was running at full speed towards the Municipal Building, where Tuttle and Johnson were just going in through the door. He reached it a moment too late; the door had shut behind the two men. Benji barked and scratched frantically on the glass. But to no avail. The glass was strong and thick, and it shut out noise. Inside the building, Benji could see Tuttle and his friend walking off down the hall and rounding a corner, out of sight. Benji barked louder, straining his throat, but nobody could hear him. He sat down on the front steps, not certain what he should do next.

Two secretaries were coming down the corridor, on the way to the front door. It was getting late; their working day was over. Benji watched the women approaching, but he couldn't hear what they were saying.

'What a day. Ol' Man Vanston's really been on a tear,' one complained.

'Tell me about it,' said her friend sarcastically. 'This is the third day in a row we've had to work late.'

They had reached the door by now, and one of them pushed it open. The instant she did so, Benji dashed between their legs and into the building, racing down the corridor.

'Hey! Come back here!' One of the women shouted.

The other laid a hand on her friend's arm. 'Oh, leave him alone. Maybe he'll hide in Vanston's office and bite him in the morning.'

Benji skidded round the corner and into the next corridor. It was empty. He slowed down and began a systematic search for Officer Tuttle. Because the hour was late, the building was nearly deserted. Benji checked into every open door, finding nothing but desks, chairs and filing cabinets. Typewriters wore their covers for the night. But Tuttle had to be here somewhere! He moved from outer offices to inner offices and back again into the corridors. Nothing. Nobody.

Suddenly Benji heard footsteps, echoing in an empty corridor. He dashed to the corner. A door shut up ahead and, at the far end of the corridor, Benji could see Officer Tuttle and his friend at a door leading out.

'Will Vanston be in in the morning?' Tuttle's voice

came to him. He was opening the door and motioning for Johnson to go through first.

'Yes.' Johnson gave Tuttle a little push through the door. 'Go ahead, I've got to lock it.' He took a set of keys from his pocket and followed his friend out of the door. It shut with an echoing thud.

Barking frantically, Benji ran down the corridor, arriving just in time to hear the lock turn. He jumped at the door, scratching and barking. No good. He dropped to all fours, sick at heart, and began to drag himself back down the hall, his head hanging in despair.

Off the corridor was a large office with a huge window, and Benji climbed up on the sill. Once more he scratched on the glass, woofing as loud as he could. But he was locked in, and nobody could hear him through the window. He laid his head on his paws, worn out.

The wastepaper basket in the office was filled to overflowing with scrap paper; some of it lay screwed up and crumpled on the carpet. Benji looked at one of the scraps. He shook his head as if to clear it. Something about a screwed up piece of paper ... Think, Benji, think! he told himself. Something tickled at the back of his mind, something about a scrap of paper ... He stood and walked over to the scrap, sniffing at it and thinking furiously.

Of course! That was it! Maybe everything wasn't lost after all! Now all he had to do was get out of here! Benji ran from corridor to corridor through the ground floor of the vast, empty building. At door after door he scratched and barked, to no avail. He had to get out! The safety of Cindy and Paul depended on him!

'O.K., Sid, let's lock it up!'

Hearing the voice, Benji's head snapped up. He ran to the corner of the hallway. There, just down the next corridor, two caretakers in overalls were turning the corner. Benji ran full-tilt towards the two men, who were heading for the front door.

'It's really been a day,' said Sid.

'Yes.' The first caretaker turned the key in the lock behind him. They were, as usual, the very last to leave. The Municipal Building was now officially shut down for the night.

Benji ran up to the locked door, his front paws scrabbling desperately at the glass, his voice raised in a series of loud barks. On the pavement outside, he could see the two caretakers bidding each other good-night. Why couldn't they hear him? The man called Sid turned down the path, but the other started round the side of the building.

Benji had to keep this man in sight; he had to get his attention somehow! He ran into the next office, which had a large window, and leaped at the glass, barking and scratching. It was no use. The caretaker passed by the window without an upward glance. Benji ran to the next office, and the next, and the next. It was never any use. He could see the man, but the man couldn't see or hear him through the thick panes of glass.

He was trapped! Trapped inside an empty building until morning! But who knew what might happen to Cindy and Paul, overnight with Mitch and his gun? He *had* to get out! What could he do?

By now the caretaker had nearly reached the back of the building, and Benji had run out of offices. All except one. This was the last office on the row. It had a drive-in window, like a box office, so that customers didn't have to come inside the building. Benji leaped to the counter and over to the drive-in window, barking furiously. With his heart in his mouth, he watched the caretaker disappear round a corner and out of sight.

Jumping up and down in a burst of last-minute energy, Benji felt his foot accidentally kick something. A switch. Benji had no idea what a switch was, or what this one did.

Suddenly the caretaker stopped in his tracks, as a very loud sound hit him in both ears. It was the sound of a dog barking, but it was louder than ten dogs. And it came from the Municipal Building, through the speaker at the drive-in window. He turned and ran back to the building.

There, in the window, stood a mongrel he'd never seen before, his tail waving furiously as he barked again and again. But how on earth had the dog turned on the microphone?

'What in blazes are you doing in there?' he yelled at Benji, whose tail wagged harder than ever. Opening a side door, the man reached down to grab the dog, but Benji had dodged between his legs and was running down the pavement as fast as he could go. Free! The caretaker watched him in wonder. How could a dog turn on a microphone?

Benji began to run, tired as he was. There was no time to rest. Soon it would be dark. If only it was still there! He dashed across streets without looking at lights or traffic; only by a whisker did he escape being run over.

He ran helter-skelter through the park. One thought alone was on his mind. If only it was still there!

At last he reached the old house on the edge of town. Everything seemed quiet; no lights shone from inside. Carefully he made his way up his 'staircase', over the roofs between the gables and in through his 'door'. Cautiously he crept through the bedroom and out on to the landing. Would it still be there?

ELEVEN

Benji crossed the upper hallway and tiptoed his way to the winding stairs. He took the stairs one at a time, with a pause on each step. He could hear his heart thudding in his body. Weary to the bone, and frightened right through, he forced himself to go on. When he reached the landing, the halfway point, he crouched down on his belly and crept quietly to his observation post, poking his little black nose through the banisters.

He could see Henry sitting in a chair downstairs, eating another one of his pudding cups. A sudden pang of hunger struck Benji like a blow, and his mouth began to water. He hadn't eaten in hours! It seemed like days! No time to think about that now. He swallowed hard and concentrated on checking out the downstairs.

Linda was walking Paul and Cindy back and forth in the foyer, back and forth. It was probably the only exercise they'd had since they'd been brought there. Now that he knew that the Chapman children were still unharmed, Benji turned his attention to the foyer carpet. Had it been picked up? What was that flash of white? Yes! There it was! The screwed up piece of paper, the first attempt at a ransom note that Riley had written and Henry had thrown aside. It was still there! It lay on the carpet, close by Linda's walking feet.

But how could Benji reach it without being seen? He stiffened as he heard Mitch's voice, coming from the sitting room.

'Will you sit down with those kids?'

'They need to move around,' Linda protested. 'They're getting restless.'

'Well, move 'em around *to* somewhere!' Mitch yelled. 'You're about to drive me crazy with that pacing back and forth!'

Linda bent down to look in the kids' faces. 'You want to go upstairs?'

Although neither Paul nor Cindy was still wearing the gags, both shook their heads.

'You're not afraid of me now?' asked Linda.

Upstairs, Benji began to creep across the landing to the lower flight of stairs, keeping his brown eyes glued to Linda and the children below.

'I don't think so,' Paul answered Linda.

'But we're afraid of this house,' added Cindy.

'Well, there's no need to be afraid of it.' Linda's tone was very sure.

Cindy nodded her head firmly. 'Uh-huh,' she said. 'Some old lady's head is in here.' She sounded as sure as Linda.

'I told you, Henry,' called Riley from the parlour.

'Shut up,' muttered Henry in return.

'Both of you shut up!' Mitch blurted. Then, louder, '*All* of you shut up!' Suddenly Mitch stormed out of the sitting room into the foyer, yelling at the top of his lungs. Benji took one look and withdrew round the corner of the landing.

'I put you people right square in the middle of a sure hundred-thousand-pound split, and all I hear is moaning because you're involved and talk about somebody's fool head floating around!'

Mitch was hopping mad, and everybody was staring at him. Benji saw his chance to sneak further downstairs, and he began to move slowly down the lower flight.

'Now, I'm sick of all of it. So *cut it*!' Mitch shouted.

'I understand that's how it all started,' said Riley's voice.

Benji froze in position. He pulled his body into the smallest possible ball and tucked it into the shadows on the next-to-the-bottom step. Riley was standing right next to him in the sitting room doorway; if he glanced down he'd be able to see Benji from that vantage point.

Mitch whirled round. 'What?'

'With the head,' said Riley, all innocence. 'Mr Powell tried to cut it.'

Mitch lost the last few remnants of his temper. Grabbing Riley by his shirt, he shouted at him. 'You be funny some other time or that head's going to have company.' He gave the shirt a final twist and let Riley go. As he turned, his eye fell on something moving in the shadows of the stairs.

'What is that?' Mitch yelled, pointing.

It was Benji!

It was now or never, no time for thinking or hesitation. Benji dashed forward like a rocket, and grabbed up the discarded note with his teeth. Then he headed back for the stairs, for the upstairs bedroom, and his 'door'.

'It's a dog!' cried Riley.

'Benji!' yelled Paul.

'Benji!' echoed Cindy.

'It's the kids' dog!' hollered Mitch. 'How'd he find us?'

Henry jumped up out of his chair, dropping his pudding cup. 'He's got the ransom note! Get him!'

Amid the shouting and the confusion, Benji tried to make it back to the stairs, but Mitch, Henry, and Riley closed in on him, closing him inside a circle. Benji skidded to a halt. He was trapped! Trapped in the foyer! The three men came closer, and Benji began to back nervously towards the corner, towards his nest. He still kept the paper clenched between his jaws. He growled menacingly.

'What d'you mean he's got the ransom note?' Mitch demanded. 'How could that be the ransom note?'

Henry tried to explain. 'It's the first try. It was sloppy, so I threw it away.'

Mitch looked daggers at Henry. If looks could kill Henry would have crumpled to the floor. Then he closed in nearer to Benji, trying to coax him in a voice heavy with false friendliness.

'Come on, fellow. Give me that piece of paper.'

Benji backed up further. He'd backed up as far as he could go. He had nowhere to turn, and Mitch was almost on top of him. With a spurt of energy, Benji made a break for it, trying to scoot around Mitch. But it didn't work. Arms swooped down and Benji felt them close around him.

'Gotcha!' yelled Mitch triumphantly.

Benji's heart sank. It was all over now. Then, when everything seemed lost, Tiffany made a rapid dash from the nest and threw her small body at Mitch, who was clutching her precious Benji. She sank her teeth viciously into Mitch's ankle, growling like a tiny tiger. With a howl of pain, Mitch dropped Benji and grabbed his ankle. Seizing the chance, Benji dashed across the floor and up the stairs, disappearing round the landing corner. He moved to the railing, and peered through the banisters at the room below.

'Where'd that one come from?' yelled Henry, pointing at Tiffany. Tiffany stood uncertainly in front of Mitch.

'You little cur! It'll be a cold day before you ever bite anyone again,' snarled Mitch at the little white dog. He cocked his foot back to kick her.

'No, don't!' yelled Cindy.

Benji stood on the landing, his heart freezing in fear. He saw the kick, a hard one, heard Tiffany yelp in pain, and saw her hurled through the air by Mitch's cruel foot. He stood there on the landing, watching in horror as she landed hard against the wall, and lay crumpled there, her head down. She was lying so still. Her small white body looked like a discarded rag. Benji felt his eyes water.

Feet were pounding on the stairs. Henry and Riley were bounding up the steps in hot pursuit of Benji. He cast another look over the banisters at Tiffany. She hadn't moved. He had to decide, *now*! Part of his very soul was lying there with Tiffany; he *had* to find out how badly she was hurt. But the other part of Benji knew duty when he saw it. He was Paul's only chance, Cindy's only hope. He decided. Darting away from his pursuer's, he headed up the stairs to the bed-room.

'There he is!' yelled Henry, taking the stairs two at a time. The boys followed Benji into the bedroom, watching in dismay as the dog, with the note still in his mouth, hopped through the broken window, out on to the porch, and over the railing to the roof. They dashed to the window and Riley began to tug at the sash.

'Hurry up, get it open!' urged Henry.

'It's stuck!' moaned Riley.

'Get out of the way!' Henry pushed Riley aside, and began to pull at the window himself.

'I tell you, it's stuck!'

Henry continued to struggle for a minute, then he gave up. 'Come on,' and he grabbed at Riley's arm, pulling him away from the window.

'I told you it was stuck,' Riley said stubbornly.

They ran to another window, and peered out, trying to see through the dusty pane of glass. 'He jumped down right out there,' said Riley, pointing to the place he'd last seen Benji.

'Come on!' urged Henry. 'Let's get downstairs, quick!'

They reached the front of the house just as Benji had crossed the arbour and was starting down the lattice work. Benji heard them coming, heard Henry yelling, 'Round this way!' His paws hit the ground at the very moment they ran into sight, and they spotted him.

'There he is!' yelled Riley. The two boys came leaping over the boxes and through the dry grass, but Benji put on all the speed his small, strong body could summon up, and Henry and Riley soon began to drop back. Exhausted and panting, his leg muscles aching, Riley wheezed 'You don't think he knows what he's doing, do you?'

'No . . .' said Henry, drawing a ragged breath '. . . but I'm not going to give him a chance to prove me wrong. Come on!' They headed back for the house, plodding slowly, looking back now and then at the blurred form running in the distance.

Benji ran as if the devil himself was after him. His ears streamed out from his head like banners pulled by the wind. The dark streets sped by him. His heart pumped twice as fast as it ever had before, but Benji was beyond caring. He was a machine with legs that ran, and with a brain that showed him nothing but fearful images.

Tiffany lying limp and unmoving against a wall. Paul shivering, his eyes filled with tears. Mitch pushing the Chapman children. Tiffany lying against the wall. Mitch's foot as it came down to kick Tiffany. Cindy crying in fear. The gun in Mitch's hand. Tiffany lying there. Tiffany. Paul. Cindy.

He kept running, the note clenched in his teeth. He reached the busiest corner in town, with traffic coming heavily from four directions. Without even waiting to check the lights, without looking, Benji hurled himself off the kerb.

Traffic poured at him from two sides. There was a screeching of tyres, a slamming of brakes, an angry shout, and a car screeched to a halt only seconds before it would have smashed Benji into pieces. Benji didn't stop. He kept running, images of terror flashing on and off in his brain, like neon signs.

Cindy crying. Tiffany lying there. Dead or alive? He didn't know. Maybe he'd never know. Paul trying to be brave. Once again, he saw Mitch's foot swing down, saw the fluffy white body hurled high in the air, crashing hard against the wall.

He crossed the lawn of the park near the courthouse square, and kept running. He dashed into traffic again, again narrowly missed getting killed, but he kept running. Now he saw Paul and Cindy alone and frightened in the foyer of the big house, gags over their mouths. He saw Cindy fall down as Mitch savagely pushed the children. And again and again he saw the crumpled white figure of little Tiffany.

He darted through the hole in the fence and across the back yard. He had lost all sense of time or place; all he knew how to do was run. Without missing a step, Benji ran up the back stairs, pushed open the screen door, and hurtled across the Chapman kitchen.

TWELVE

'Yes,' said Floyd. 'One of them seems to be working fine now, but I've still got nothing on the other one.' He gestured at the newly installed telephones.

'Thank you very much. That's very thoughtful,' Dr Chapman said to someone.

Benji raced down the last few feet of hallway towards the living room and the voices. Then he stopped in the doorway, unable to believe his eyes. The pretty young girl Dr Chapman was thanking was Linda Sue! Here!

'Well,' Linda was saying, 'I just wanted to call and see if there was anything I could do ...' She broke off as she spotted Benji.

Benji crouched a little in fear, and began backing away. Why was she here?

'Mary, it's that dog again!' called Lieutenant Samuels.

Benji backed further down the hall, but Linda kept following him, a smile pasted to her face. 'Isn't he cute?' and she held out her hand for the note in his mouth.

'Where's the ransom note?' yelled Floyd, remembering his last encounter with Benji.

'I have it,' said the FBI man.

'Mary! Please get him out of here!' Dr Chapman's voice was very angry.

Mary bustled up to get Benji, as Linda reached over for the note.

'Let me see what you've got there, doggy,' purred Linda.

'Benji! Come here to me! This minute!' snapped Mary, furious. But Linda had reached him first, and she pulled the note from his mouth. Baring his teeth, Benji snapped at her just as Mary grabbed him and lifted him off the ground. He never took his eyes off Linda or the note.

'Benji! Stop it!' Mary scolded him loudly, giving him a shake. 'What's the matter with you?'

Linda had read the note; it was the one she'd been sent to get, no matter how. 'Hmm,' she said casually. 'Somebody's old grocery list.' Without being obvious, she slid the note into her handbag. 'Well, I have to be going,' she called brightly. Benji never took his eyes off her, and a low growl issued from his throat.

'I'll show you to the door,' said Dr Chapman. They followed, holding Benji, out of the living room. Mary started down the hall to the kitchen, Linda and the Doctor headed for the front door.

'Thank you for coming, Linda Sue,' Mary called over her shoulder. 'I'm sorry about the dog.'

'Don't worry about it.' Linda shook her pretty head, a look of relief on her face.

'It was nice of you to come over,' said Dr Chapman. 'We appreciate it.'

Benji was riding on Mary's bosom, held tightly in her arms, but able to look back down the hallway to the front door. His intelligent brown eyes were fixed on Linda and her open bag. She was holding it by the long strap and it was close to the floor.

'I wanted to,' Linda was saying. 'I wasn't even sure you'd remember me, but I wanted to come.' Benji and the note were getting further and further apart, the closer Mary came to the kitchen. He squirmed in Mary's grip. Once she put him outside the back door, and Linda left by the front, it would be too late to save the children.

'Of course I remember you,' said Dr Chapman. 'A few years can't erase a pretty face like yours.'

'Thank you.' Linda showed her dimples, but she was plainly eager to be gone. 'Again, if there's anything we can do, just let us know. There's always someone around the house.'

'Say hello to your mother and father for us, Linda Sue,' called Mary, stopping for one moment.

'I'll do it.' Linda had her hand on the doorknob. Benji's eyes narrowed in agony. The bag! The bag! 'And they send their love,' chirped Linda. Mary turned towards the kitchen again.

'Now remember,' Linda Sue was saying as the front door swung open, 'Anything ...' She broke off suddenly at a cry from Mary. Benji had whirled round and bitten her on the hand. It wasn't a deep bite, but a bite just the same, and painful. With a yell, Mary dropped Benji and he made a beeline for Linda, dashing down the corridor.

'Mary! What's the matter?' called Dr Chapman.

'He bit me!' said Mary. Surprise and shock were written all over her face.

Dr Chapman saw Benji barrelling down the hallway and reached out for him before he could get to Linda. 'Hold it right there!' he shouted.

But Benji snapped at him and the Doctor jerked back as Benji made a leap for Linda's bag. The frightened girl tried to beat him off, but Benji grabbed it in his teeth and yanked it out of her hands. Linda gave a scream that turned into a wail of dismay, as she saw Benji dart through Dr Chapman's hands and head back down the hall.

Floyd made a running dive and got one hand on the strap. For a minute, officer and dog struggled for ownership, then Floyd, with a sudden yank pulled it away from Benji. But as the dog lost his grip the handbag went flying through the air, landing across the room. It crashed against the far wall and the contents spilled out everywhere. Lipstick, keys, mirror, money ... and the *note*!'

Benji scampered across the room in a flash and picked the note up in his teeth again. With Linda chasing him frantically, he made a dash for safety, the only safety he knew ... Mary's arms.

'Come back here, dog! Give that to me!' shouted Linda.

Mary stood in the hallway, gingerly holding her bitten hand, but as Benji ran towards her and leaped into her arms, she had no choice but to catch him.

'*What* is the matter with you?' she demanded, puzzlement in her voice as the dog pushed the note into her hand.

'That's mine! Give it here!' Linda was almost screaming.

But Mary was unfolding the note with one hand and reading the words on the paper. Her eyes widened, and she whistled softly. 'Or ... I ... should ... say what is the matter with *us*?'

'Give that to me!' Linda stretched her hands out, trying to pull the note from Mary's hand. But Mary held it firmly. She set Benji down gently and rushed down the hallway, her face clouded with concern.

'Dr Chapman! Lieutenant Samuels! Look at this!' Linda ran after her, still reaching out for the crumpled piece of paper.

'No! It's mine! Give it to me!' Suddenly, she began to cry, breaking down in huge sobs. 'Please,' she moaned.

Dr Chapman took the note and Samuels looked over his shoulder as both men read the contents.

'It's another ransom note,' said the detective. Over his shoulder, he called to the FBI man. 'Payton, are you sure that you've got the original?'

'Right here,' said Murrah. He pulled a slip of lavender paper from his coat pocket.

Dr Chapman looked slowly up at Linda, his eyes narrowed in icy rage. 'Where are Paul and Cindy?' he demanded of the sobbing girl.

'I don't know!' she wept.

But Benji knew. He began to bark, and bark, and bark. They all turned to look at him, and slowly the truth began to dawn ...

He was exhausted; he'd been running all day. His legs ached, his breath came panting, but his heart was lighter. For, running behind him, were Dr Chapman, the police detective, the FBI man, Floyd and the other officers, Bob Felding, and Mr Harvey. Two of the officers held walkie-talkies and were directing a support team over them.

And, huffing and puffing, bringing up the rear, came Mary. She had refused to be left behind. Not when Benji was leading the way.

THIRTEEN

Most of the light had faded from the summer sky; Riley had lit a few old candles and placed them around. They gave the eerie old place an even creepier look, and they made the three men nervous and jumpy.

'We should've done what I said and cleared out of here an hour ago,' complained Henry. 'And I say we don't wait any longer.'

'We're giving her ten more minutes,' snapped Mitch. 'Now sit down and shut up!'

Riley stood by the window near the front door, peering out through the drape. 'In ten minutes it's sure going to be dark in here,' he said nervously.

'It didn't work, Mitch! She's not coming!' Henry sounded near panic. 'Now we've got to get out of here and get to a safer place. *Now!*'

'I'm for that,' agreed Riley.

'Sit down!' Mitch commanded.

The trio waited a few minutes more in a silence that was heavy with growing tension. Then Henry stood up; he had reached a decision. 'Forget it!' he shouted. 'We're going now! You either capture us or come on!'

Mitch could tell from the expression on his face that Henry would take no more orders from him. It would have to be force or surrender.

He thought hard for a minute, then shrugged, an expression of weariness on his dark face. 'All right. We'll go. But not half-cocked! Let's plan it out.'

They were slowing down a little, running out of breath. Benji would get too far ahead of them; then he'd have to turn and wait in the growing darkness, barking at them so they wouldn't get lost.

Lieutenant Samuels hadn't been this far on foot since his recruit days. He missed his specially equipped unmarked patrol car. 'Mary,' he complained to the housekeeper, who huffed and puffed beside him, 'Can't you ask him how much further?'

And Benji was beginning to get anxious, too. It was taking so long to get there! If only humans had four feet like dogs! He barked impatiently.

Mitch, Henry, and Riley gathered round the map on the table. The candlelight made a strange pattern of wavy lines on the map, and they had to bend close to make it out clearly.

'You're sure about this place?' asked Mitch.

'Positive,' Henry replied. 'And there'll be nobody around there for miles at this time of year.'

Mitch nodded decisively; he was still in charge. 'O.K. Pack 'em up,' he said, nodding at the children, who sat petrified, afraid to think about what might happen to them next.

Benji's little group straggled on through the dark, following Benji's short cuts. Most of the route consisted of alley ways and narrow dirt paths, just right for a smallish dog, but rough going for full-grown humans. They often stumbled; Benji kept barking at them to hurry.

'We must be getting close,' said Samuels. 'See if you can keep him quiet, Mary.'

They were gagged again, so they couldn't cry out for help. Without Linda there to stop him, Mitch handled Paul and Cindy roughly, pushing them towards the side door of the old house and shouting at them when they stumbled. Henry and Riley led the way, and Mitch followed through the door with one child under each arm. Henry looked around him on all sides. He could see nothing in the darkness. He set off, Mitch following.

'Don't move a muscle,' said Lieutenant Samuels.

Mitch froze as he felt the ice-cold barrel of a pistol against each side of his forehead. His eyes darted from side to side. Samuels and Floyd were flanking him, guns drawn and pressed against Mitch's head. Payton stepped out of concealment behind a bush and trained his gun on Henry.

Riley turned to run back into the house, but the second plain clothes man stepped out from the porch, gun in hand.

'Now put 'em down real easy,' Samuels ordered. Mitch eased Cindy and Paul gently to the ground and

Floyd deftly removed their gags.

'Here, I'll get these for you,' he said. 'Are you O.K.?'

Unable to speak for the moment, they could only nod.

'That's good,' said Floyd. 'There you go.'

The detective lieutenant was moving Mitch, Riley, and Henry away from the house and out on to the street. Coming up the driveway at a run were Mary, Dr Chapman, and the others.

'Paul! Cindy!'

'Daddy! Mary!'

'Benji!'

'RRRRRRRRRRRRRRRwooooooffffff!'

It was a happy group that left Dr Chapman's office. Benji ran out of the office door first, barking cheerfully and turning around often to encourage the others to hurry. Tiffany came next, hobbling slowly; on one of her hind legs a large cast proved Dr Chapman's skill, even with dogs. Her white fur had been brushed to a gleam and she smiled at Benji, a secret smile.

Cindy came out behind her. 'You should've seen her, Daddy,' she grinned. 'She was really brave.'

'So was Benji,' said Paul defending his favourite.

Dr Chapman followed Mary out of his office, locking the door behind him. He smiled lovingly at his children, then turned the smile on the two dogs.

'We owe them both a lot. There's no doubt about that.'

'Would you say they're kind of heroes?' asked Cindy.

Dr Chapman started down the path from the door. 'I'd say they were definitely heroes.'

'You left a light on,' Mary pointed out.

As Dr Chapman turned back to switch off the light, Paul and Cindy whispered quickly, while Mary watched them with a knowing smile on her plump face.

'Well, if we owe them a lot and they're heroes,' she tackled her father as he came out again, 'it wouldn't be right to send them out in the streets, would it?'

'Especially when one's a *wounded* hero,' Paul chimed in.

Dr Chapman shot a sharp wise look at Mary, who said nothing, but didn't try to hide the wide grin that tugged the corners of her mouth upward.

'I don't know, Mary, what do you think? Have you ever known any heroes that got turned out into the streets?'

Mary pretended to think about it. 'Not too many,' she admitted finally.

'Then can they go home with us?' pressed Paul.

Dr Chapman shook his head slightly and pursed his lips, his brow creasing in a mock frown. 'Oh, I'm afraid we might get too attached to them by then,' he said. He watched the faces of both his children fall in dismay and disappointment. 'So maybe,' the doctor continued, 'We should just plan on them staying for good . . . unless they get tired of us.'

With squeals of joy, Paul and Cindy ran to their father and hugged him hard; then they turned to Mary, who was laughing, and hugged her too. Jumping up and down, they couldn't stop the flow of their happiness; it seemed to the children that they had never been so happy before.

Cindy bent down and picked little Tiffany up in

her arms. 'Come on, Benji,' she said. 'We're going home.'

Home! The word sounded sweet in Benji's ears. It brought up images of soft beds; he was lying at the foot of Paul's bed and Tiffany was sleeping on Cindy's. Suddenly home seemed to mean Mary's lap and a warm kitchen and an end to roaming. He felt a brief pang for the single life, but somewhere inside some canine instinct told him that his roaming days were over and that his homing days were about to begin. He trotted happily down the street at Paul's side, and he felt he belonged there.

'Do we have to build a fence?' Paul asked his father.

'No fences,' said Dr Chapman.

'What about all those germs and diseases and stuff?' his son wanted to know.

'Well,' said Dr Chapman slowly, 'let's just say my values have been shifted around?'

'Do you understand that?' Cindy asked her brother.

'I think it means he made a mistake.'

Mary grinned. 'I have a feeling that Benji will be sticking pretty close to home. At least until Tiffany can travel better.'

'By then,' declared Cindy, 'we can love him so much he'll *want* to stay.'

Dr Chapman looked fondly at his son and daughter. 'I don't know anyone more qualified to do that than you two.' He put his arms around both of them and gave them a big hug, then the three of them walked down the street together, Cindy with Tiffany in her arms.

Benji fell back a few steps to walk with Mary. She grinned down at his sturdy body and shaggy, intelligent face. 'Benji, didn't I always tell you he was a pretty nice man?' Benji barked a yes. 'Just a little stubborn sometimes. Never really bad, mind you ...'

'RRRRRRwooooff!' said Benji.

And they all walked off through the darkness towards the house waiting for them. The blinking traffic lights and neon signs seemed to celebrate their happiness.

TARGET STORY BOOKS

Adventure

Gordon Boshell
113918 THE BLACK MERCEDES 60p

114043 THE MILLION POUND RANSOM 60p

117468 THE MENDIP MONEY-MAKERS 60p

Animal Stories

Molly Burkett
118502 FOXES, OWLS AND ALL (NF) (illus) 70p

111567 THAT MAD, BAD BADGER ... (NF) (illus) 35p

Constance Taber Colby
109899 A SKUNK IN THE FAMILY (NF) (illus) 45p

I. J. Edmonds
20011X LASSIE: THE WILD MOUNTAIN TRAIL 60p

G. D. Griffiths
113675 ABANDONED! (illus) 50p

David Gross
117549 THE BADGERS OF BADGER HILL (illus) 50p

Michael Maguire
**118774 MYLOR, THE MOST POWERFUL
HORSE IN THE WORLD** (illus) 60p

Joyce Stranger
11017X THE SECRET HERDS (illus) 45p

110099 THE HARE AT DARK HOLLOW (illus) 40p

Mystery And Suspense

Ruth M. Arthur
111648 THE AUTUMN GHOSTS (illus) 50p

111729 THE CANDLEMAS MYSTERY (illus) 45p*

Tim Dinsdale
**105915 THE STORY OF THE
LOCH NESS MONSTER** (illus) 50p

Leonard Gribble
**104285 FAMOUS HISTORICAL
MYSTERIES** (NF) (illus) 50p

Alfred Hitchcock (Editor)
**117387 ALFRED HITCHCOCK'S TALES OF
TERROR AND SUSPENSE** 60p

Mollie Hunter
113756 THE WALKING STONES (illus) 45p*

Freya Littledale
**107357 GHOSTS AND SPIRITS OF
MANY LANDS** (illus) 50p

†For sale in Britain and Ireland only.
*Not for sale in Canada.
♦ Film & T.V. tie-ins.

COOKERY

0352	Star	
395613	Hazel Adair and Peter Ling **THE CROSSROADS COOKBOOK**	70p ♦
0426	Tandem	
089502	Jill McWilliams **JILL McWILLIAMS BOOK OF FREEZING**	80p*
085981	**THE VIETNAMESE COOK BOOK** Hoang Huu Can	75p
0426	Hanau Distribution	
087070	**THE HAPPY COOKER** Marilyn Hayes & Al Lerman	95p*

TARGET STORY BOOKS

'Doctor Who'

0426

200098	Terrance Dicks **DOCTOR WHO AND THE** **HORROR OF FANG ROCK**		60p
108663	Brian Hayles **DOCTOR WHO AND THE ICE WARRIORS**		60p
110412	Terrance Dicks **DOCTOR WHO AND THE LOCH NESS** **MONSTER**		60p
118936	Philip Hinchcliffe **DOCTOR WHO AND THE MASQUE** **OF MANDRAGORA**		60p
116909	Terrance Dicks **DOCTOR WHO AND THE MUTANTS**		60p
116828	Terrance Dicks **DOCTOR WHO AND THE PLANET** **OF EVIL**		60p
116666	Terrance Dicks **DOCTOR WHO AND THE PYRAMIDS** **OF MARS**		60p
11308X	Malcolm Hulke **DOCTOR WHO AND THE** **SEA-DEVILS**	(illus)	40p
116585	Philip Hinchcliffe **DOCTOR WHO AND THE SEEDS** **OF DOOM**		50p
110331	Malcolm Hulke **DOCTOR WHO AND THE SPACE WAR**		60p
119738	Terrance Dicks **DOCTOR WHO AND THE TALONS OF** **WENG - CHIANG**		60p
110846	Terrance Dicks **DOCTOR WHO AND THE WEB OF FEAR**		60p
113241	Bill Strutton **DOCTOR WHO AND THE ZARBI**	(illus)	60p
114477	Terrance Dicks **THE DOCTOR WHO MONSTER BOOK**	(illus)	50p
200012	**THE SECOND DOCTOR WHO** **MONSTER BOOK**	(Colour illus)	70p
118421	Terrance Dicks **THE DOCTOR WHO DINOSAUR BOOK**		75p
116151	Terrance Dicks and Malcolm Hulke **THE MAKING OF DOCTOR WHO**		60p

TARGET STORY BOOKS

'Doctor Who'

200020	DOCTOR WHO DISCOVERS PREHISTORIC ANIMALS	(NF)	(illus)	75p
200039	DOCTOR WHO DISCOVERS SPACE TRAVEL	(NF)	(illus)	75p
200047	DOCTOR WHO DISCOVERS STRANGE AND MYSTERIOUS CREATURES	(NF)	(illus)	75p
20008X	DOCTOR WHO DISCOVERS THE STORY OF EARLY MAN	(NF)	(illus)	75p
200136	DOCTOR WHO DISCOVERS THE CONQUERORS	(NF)	(illus)	75p

Ian Marter
116313 DOCTOR WHO AND THE ARK IN SPACE 50p

Terrance Dicks
116747 DOCTOR WHO AND THE BRAIN OF MORBIUS 50p*

Terrance Dicks
110250 DOCTOR WHO AND THE CARNIVAL OF MONSTERS 50p

Malcolm Hulke
11471X DOCTOR WHO AND THE CAVE MONSTERS 60p

Terrance Dicks
117034 DOCTOR WHO AND THE CLAWS OF AXOS 50p*

David Whitaker
113160 DOCTOR WHO AND THE CRUSADERS (illus) 60p

Brian Hayles
114981 DOCTOR WHO AND THE CURSE OF PELADON 60p

Gerry Davis
114639 DOCTOR WHO AND THE CYBERMEN 60p

Barry Letts
113322 DOCTOR WHO AND THE DAEMONS (illus) 40p

David Whitaker
101103 DOCTOR WHO AND THE DALEKS 60p

Terrance Dicks
11244X DOCTOR WHO AND THE DALEK INVASION OF EARTH 60p

Terrance Dicks
119657 DOCTOR WHO AND THE DEADLY ASSASSIN 60p

Terrance Dicks
200063 DOCTOR WHO AND THE FACE OF EVIL 60p

Terrance Dicks
112601 DOCTOR WHO AND THE GENESIS OF THE DALEKS 60p

† For sale in Britain and Ireland only.
* Not for sale in Canada.
◆ Film & T.V. tie-ins.

Wyndham Books are obtainable from many booksellers and newsagents. If you have any difficulty please send purchase price plus postage on the scale below to:

Wyndham Cash Sales
P.O. Box 11
Falmouth
Cornwall

While every effort is made to keep prices low, it is sometimes necessary to increase prices at short notice. Wyndham Books reserve the right to show new retail prices on covers which may differ from those advertised in the text or elsewhere.

Postage and Packing Rate

UK: 22p for the first book, plus 10p per copy for each additional book ordered to a maximum charge of 82p. **BFPO and Eire:** 22p for the first book, plus 10p per copy for the next 6 books and thereafter 4p per book. **Overseas:** 30p for the first book and 10p per copy for each additional book.

These charges are subject to Post Office charge fluctuations.